Eat Your Poison, Dear

Other Aladdin Paperbacks by James Howe

Stage Fright

What Eric Knew

Coming Soon

Morgan's Zoo

A Night without Stars

EAT YOUR POISON, DEAR

A Sebastian Barth Mystery by

JAMES HOWE

Aladdin Paperbacks

First Aladdin Paperbacks edition September 1995
Copyright © 1986 by James Howe

Aladdin Paperbacks
An imprint of Simon & Schuster
Children's Publishing Division
1230 Avenue of the Americas
New York, NY 10020

Also available in an Atheneum Books for Young
Readers edition
Designed by Mary Ahern

Manufactured in the United States of America
10

The Library of Congress has cataloged the hardcover
edition as follows:

Howe, James.   Eat your poison, dear.

(Sebastian Barth mysteries ; bk. 3)
SUMMARY: Young sleuth Sebastian and three friends
probe the mystery of a poisoning in their school
cafeteria.
[1. Schools—Fiction.   2. Mystery and detective
stories]   I. Title.
PZ7.H83727Eat   1986   [Fic]   86-3582
ISBN 0-689-31206-7
ISBN 0-689-80339-7 (Aladdin pbk.)

To
Lee & Susan
Howe

Eat Your Poison, Dear

1 ADAM WELLS couldn't believe his eyes.

"What *is* that garbage?" he asked Sebastian Barth, as the two boys inched their way along the cafeteria line.

"Precisely," said Sebastian.

"Its odor doesn't even give us a clue," Milo Groot piped up. Milo, younger and shorter than most of his fellow eighth-graders, had to pipe up if he wanted to be noticed.

"That's not entirely true," said Sebastian. "I'm picking up whiffs of canned tomato sauce and cider."

"Sounds delicious," Adam said. "Why didn't I pack a sandwich?"

"From the look of the yellow stuff under the red stuff," Sebastian went on, "I'd say we're having apple lasagna."

"Apple lasagna," said Adam. "I think I'll pretend I packed a sandwich. And that I ate it already."

Just then, Jason Bruxter and Brad West fell into line behind Milo and began playing demolition derby with their trays.

"The Devil Riders have arrived," Milo muttered

[3]

under his breath, "Pembroke Middle School's latest and greatest case of arrested development."

Sebastian didn't respond. He was watching the cafeteria manager ladle the mystery food onto a plate and start to hand it to Adam. Suddenly, she yanked it back.

"What's the matter, Miss Swille?" Sebastian asked. "Has today's lunch been recalled?"

"Oh, Sebastian," Miss Swille said, "you're such a tease. I forgot Adam's string beans, is all." Heaping the plate with limp, khaki-colored vegetables, she returned it to Adam, and said, "Now eat your string beans, dear. They're full of potassium."

"What exactly *are* we eating today?" Sebastian asked. "Other than the potassium, I mean."

"It's a little recipe all my own. Apple lasagna." Miss Swille scraped the bottom of the bin, not forgetting the string beans this time, and advised Sebastian to eat them all up. Sebastian promised to try, as Miss Swille turned away and addressed her student volunteer. "Harlan, dear, we need more lasagna. Why, I never imagined it would be this popular."

"Me neither," said the tall, gangly boy in the cut-off denim vest. "And, Miss Swille, my name is Harley." Spotting Jason and Brad in line, he gave them the thumbs-up sign, then went off to get a fresh pan of lasagna from the oven.

" 'Eat your string beans, dear,' " Adam said mockingly as he and Sebastian seated themselves.

[4]

"How about 'eat your poison, dear'? You know something, Sebastian? This school should serve insurance policies with lunch, I'm not kidding."

Sebastian laughed. "Remember the food riot last spring?"

"That was so great! It must have taken them a month to get all the melted cheese off the overhead lights."

"Yeah, well, I'll tell you one thing. Miss Swille hasn't dared make tunafish dreamboats since then."

"Listen," said Adam, "she was making them every week. No wonder there was a —" He stopped himself when he saw Milo Groot coming up behind Sebastian.

The spiky-haired ten-year-old held his tray in one hand, an open book in the other. "There aren't any empty tables," Milo said. "Is it all right if I sit with you, Barth?"

"It's a free country," Sebastian said.

Adam groaned. "Apple lasagna and Milo Groot. The perfect lunch." Trying to shut out this latest development, he turned to Sebastian and picked up on his earlier train of thought. "Seriously, Sebastian, sometimes I can't decide if Miss Swille really likes kids and is helping us grow up to be big and strong by putting our stomachs through some kind of basic training, or she hates us all and is slowly killing us off."

"Oh, it isn't so bad," Sebastian said. "My mom

tells me Miss Swille knows a lot about nutrition. So I guess we're well fed."

"So are hogs," said Adam.

The sound of raucous laughter at a nearby table drew the boys' attention.

"I still can't believe it," Adam said, watching Jason Bruxter and Brad West squirt milk at each other through their straws.

"You mean 'Breeze' and 'Biker'?"

Adam grunted. "Yeah. Where'd they come up with those names, anyway? 'Jason' and 'Brad' were always good enough, until Harley came along."

Milo looked up from his book. "Harley chose the names, I'm sure. Picked them out of a dictionary, perhaps. Just getting to the B's was probably the most reading he's ever done. Personally, I think the whole thing's disgusting."

Sebastian and Adam exchanged a look.

"School is no place for gangs like the Devil Riders," Milo continued. "Mr. Hogan shouldn't allow it. They're noisy and disruptive, and they dress like fugitives from a reform school."

"Why don't you tell Harley what you think?" Adam asked.

Milo smiled. "I'm going to do better than that. I've written an editorial in this week's paper. Soon, the whole school—*and* Mr. Hogan—will know my views."

[6]

"I guess as editor of the school paper, you can do whatever you want," Sebastian said. "I'd just watch out for Harley, if I were you."

"Harley doesn't scare me," Milo said, and he took another bite of apple lasagna.

"Hey, Sebastian!"

Sebastian looked across the room to see Ricky Siddons waving a fork. "This stuff is the pits, right? What do you say? Want to start another riot?"

Mrs. Evans, the cafeteria monitor that day, scowled ferociously. "It isn't *that* bad," Sebastian said. "I ate it."

"Yeah," said Ricky. "So did your friend Milo. And look at him."

Everybody turned to Milo, whose face was growing pale.

"You all right?" Sebastian asked.

"Of course I'm all right," Milo said. "I just ate too fast, that's all. I'll feel better once I . . . once I . . ."

"Throw up," Adam said. And on cue, Milo Groot did just that, to the sound of laughing and cheering throughout the cafeteria. Mrs. Evans ran to his side, clapping her hands as she did. "That's enough," she cried. "Stop it, boys and girls. It isn't funny."

Watching Milo, Sebastian drained his milk carton, then picked up his tray and commented, "You know, another interesting thing about Miss Swille's food is that it doesn't look any different after you've eaten it."

2 ON THEIR WAY out of the cafeteria, the two boys bumped into Sebastian's friend, David Lepinsky.

"Where are you going?" Sebastian said. "Don't you have math now?"

"I work in the office this period on Tuesdays," said David. "I'm bringing these posters to Miss Swille."

"Let's see," Sebastian said.

"Brownnose," said Adam.

"I am not. I get credit for helping out in the office."

"You work there every day?"

"Yep. Different periods, and sometimes for only fifteen minutes. But every day. I like it. They forget I'm there, so I get to hear all kinds of good stuff."

"I think we're in for more than apple lasagna," said Sebastian, studying a rolled-out poster. "Listen. 'Apple-cadabra. Good health doesn't happen by magic. It just seems that way when it tastes as delicious as this favorite fall-time fruit. Enjoy the magic of apples all month long at your school cafeteria.' I

[9]

shudder to think of what Miss Swille will come up with next. And October has just begun."

"It smells like she's already at her cauldron," David said.

Adam smirked. "That's Milo," he said.

"What happened?" David asked. "Was he sick?"

"Let's just say that Miss Swille's cooking didn't agree with him."

"It doesn't agree with anybody," David said. "But nobody's gotten sick from it before."

"Well, maybe he was poisoned," Sebastian said.

"Who'd want to poison Milo Groot?" David asked.

There was a moment of silence. Then the three boys broke out laughing, as together they cried, "Everybody!"

3 "*MES AMIS, MES AMIS!*" Monsieur Hameauvert shouted over the din of arriving students. "*Attention, s'il vous plaît! Maintenant,
nous—vous m'entendez, mes amis? Écoutez-moi, s'il
vous plaît! Écoutez-moi! Maintenant, nous . . . nous—*
Listen up!"

The room fell silent.

"Is it too early in the year to be speaking
French?" said Monsieur Hameauvert. "Must I use
English to be understood?"

"Wouldn't hurt," Harley mumbled. A handful
of students snickered.

"*Pardon*," Monsieur Hameauvert said. "What
did you say, Edouard?"

"I didn't say nothing," said Harley. He slouched
over his desk, studying the cover of his new motorcycle
magazine. "And my name is Harley," he said softly.

"*Mais oui*," the teacher said. "Harley. But Harley is not your real name, is it, Monsieur Davidson?
It is a nickname, an affectation, as it were. Your real
name is Edward. And here in French class, we use the
French equivalents to our names, do we not? Edward
becomes Edouard."

"And Green-burg becomes Hameau-vert," Harley said to his magazine.

"Monsieur Davidson, I am having some difficulty hearing you. Perhaps you would be so kind as to move to the front of the room. We have an empty seat here, right across from my desk. *Où est* Monsieur Groot today? Does anyone know where Milo is?"

Walking toward the front of the room, Harley said, "He puked at lunch. Sorry, Mr. Hameauvert, I don't know how to say that in French."

The class erupted in laughter as Monsieur Hameauvert turned to the board and wrote on it:

Vomir = To puke

"The chalk awaits, Edouard. Please come to the board and conjugate this verb. I will then ask you to use it in several sentences, varying its tense. Class, take out your notebooks and conjugate along with Monsieur Davidson."

"Geez," Adam whispered to Sebastian, "Greenburg is really coming down on Harley today."

"I think the only one who doesn't get on Harley is Miss Swille," said Sebastian. "And maybe his mother."

"I heard his mother has tattoos," Corrie Wingate whispered from the desk behind Sebastian's.

"Oh, yeah?" said Adam. "Where?"

Corrie started to giggle. "*I* don't know," she said, feeling her cheeks grow hot.

Monsieur Hameauvert looked up from his desk.

[1 2]

"If you are going to giggle, Mademoiselle Wingate," he said, "please do so in French. If you do not know how to manage that feat, perhaps you should pay attention so that you might learn."

"Sorry," Corrie said. "*Je regrette.*"

"*Merci.*"

Corrie turned, red-faced, to her work.

The only sounds for the next few minutes were the scratching of pencil on paper, the squeaking of chalk on blackboard and the turning of pages, as Phil Greenburg (he was Monsieur Hameauvert only to his French students) studied the magazine he'd picked up from Harley's desk. Sebastian didn't notice David enter the room. But he did see him hand a note to the French teacher and wiggle his ears while it was read.

"*Merci bien,* David."

"*Il n'y a pas de quoi!*" David replied. He smiled at Sebastian, and left the room. Sebastian smiled to himself. His friend just couldn't resist an opportunity to show off.

"I hope you are all properly shamed," said Monsieur Hameauvert, "to hear a seventh-grader converse so easily in French." He turned to Harley at the board and said, "You may sit down now, Edouard. And plan on keeping this seat for the rest of the week. I have just learned that our friend Milo has the flu. I expect it will be some time before he rejoins us. Until then, you and I shall be keeping close company." He put the motorcycle magazine away in his desk, and said,

"Now, let us try a sentence using the infinitive. First in French, then the English. Edouard?"

Harley looked down at his empty desk top. *"Cette classe de française me fait vomir,"* he said. "French class makes me puke."

4 "WHAT A DAY," Corrie Wingate said, kicking at the leaves as she walked. There was a tone in her voice Sebastian hadn't heard before. "School was never like this in Troy."

"What do you mean?" David asked. "Didn't kids throw up where you used to live?"

"I'm not talking about Milo. Besides, I was already out of the cafeteria when that happened. I was thinking more about French class and what happened after."

"Oh," said Sebastian. He waved to Jason and Brad, who were walking on the other side of the street. They didn't wave back.

"Creeps," David muttered. "What are they doing here anyway? Why aren't they on their bus?"

"They're probably headed for the Mobil station to hang out with Harley. They go there a lot these days. You know what Adam calls them? 'Greasers in designer jeans.' "

David laughed. "He's pretty unhappy about them, isn't he?"

"Can you blame him? The poor guy goes off to New Mexico to spend the summer with his grandparents, and when he gets back home his best friends don't want anything to do with him anymore."

"That's lousy," David said. "But what I don't understand is why they became friends with Harley."

"Nobody does."

Corrie sighed.

"What's wrong?" Sebastian asked.

"Why did Monsieur Hameauvert have to pick on me today?" Corrie said. "Other people get away with giggling. I get called on it every time."

"You're just sensitive because you're new," said Sebastian. "Believe me, with Harley in the class, Greenburg isn't going to lose sleep over you. Besides, you do all your work and you get good grades. He won't flunk you because you giggle once in a while."

"You're probably right. But you know what else happened? Mr. Hogan called me into his office this afternoon. He said he and Mr. Turman had talked, and they just don't think it's safe to let a girl play football on the boys' team. I told him I don't see why the Panthers had to be a *boys'* team anyway. Every sport, I said, should be for every kid, whatever their sex."

"Boy, girl, or other," said Sebastian.

"Very funny. You know what I'm talking about. It's discrimination, Sebastian. Even if you don't understand, your mother does. Ask her."

"I don't have to ask her. My mother raised me

[1 6]

and her consciousness at the same time. I'm pretty en-lightened about these things."

"I wish other people were."

"I don't think girls should play football at all," said David.

Corrie sighed again. "See what I mean?" she said.

"Don't give up," Sebastian told her, putting his arm lightly around her shoulders. "There's always tomorrow."

"Gee, Annie," said David, "is this the part where you hug the big dog and start singing?"

"No," Sebastian said. "This is the part where you hug your books and start running."

By the time the three friends reached the corner, they were out of breath and laughing. Stopping to help pick up David's fallen books, Corrie said, "I feel better already. You're right, Sebastian, tomorrow's another day."

5

THE BELL RANG LOUDLY. It was ten forty, the beginning of third period.

"Wow, listen to this." Adam folded back the editorial page of the *Paragon* and read aloud: " 'Ganging Up on Education.' "

"Milo always had a way with headlines," said Sebastian, picking at the knot of his shop apron. "Keep reading. Mr. Branch'll probably be late as usual."

" 'When I arrived for the first day of school this year,' " Adam read, " 'I could tell right away something was different. I kept checking the time. No, I don't mean consulting a watch to be sure I was in the right class at the right hour. I mean looking at the calendar. I could have sworn it was 1957! Everywhere I looked, I saw slicked-back hair and motorcycle boots, greasy denim jackets with their sleeves hacked off and grinning skulls emblazoned on their backs.'

" 'I admit I haven't seen any switchblades, but what I have seen is bad enough. It isn't 1957, and even if it were, gangs have no place in the hallowed corridors of Academe!' "

"Oh, brother. Leave it to Milo to call school halls the 'hallowed corridors of Academe.'"

"Really," said Adam. "Let's see. Where was I? Oh, yeah. 'These dark and gloomy prophets of another time are a pestilence that must be scourged from our midst before they become such a commonplace that we take them for granted, like dandruff.'"

Sebastian stifled a laugh.

"'The gangs that have been allowed to infiltrate our beloved school must be banished! We are granted the privilege to learn and to flourish in these our formative years, and no third-rate company production of *West Side Story* should be allowed to stand in our way.' Whew! Well, there's one good thing about this editorial."

"What's that?"

"Harley's too dumb to understand it."

Sebastian shook his head. "Harley's a lot smarter than he lets on," he said.

Adam put down the newspaper and picked up his apron. "Well, all I can say is it's a good thing Milo's out of school today. His getting the flu is sort of like the governor reprieving his death sentence. Once Harley finds out—"

"But, as you say, Harley won't understand the editorial," said a voice from behind the boys. "Mr. Hogan will, however."

"Milo!" Sebastian said, turning around. "What happened to the flu?"

"Didn't want to keep the electric chair waiting, huh, Milo?" Adam cracked.

"I'm not worried about Harley, if that's what you mean," said Milo, strapping on his glasses. "And the flu's gone."

"One of those twenty-four hour bugs?" Sebastian said.

"I guess. Or something I ate," said Milo, as Mr. Branch threw open the door and asked, "Has the bell rung yet?"

6 "WHERE'S YOUR LUNCH?" Adam asked, as he and Sebastian entered the cafeteria.

"Awaiting within," said Sebastian.

"You're kidding. You're going to buy hot lunch again? After yesterday?"

"I like mysteries."

Adam grunted. "I don't know how she gets away with it. You know my cousin Shawn?" Sebastian nodded. "He went to school here five years ago, and he says Miss Swille was making the same weird concoctions then. And nobody did anything about it. I'll tell you the truth, Sebastian, and I'm not kidding. I think she's paying somebody off. I smell a scandal."

"Smells more like apple chili dogs to me."

"Please. Even Miss Swille wouldn't go *that* far."

Later, as Sebastian finished off the last of his apple chili dog, Adam said, "You want to know how it makes me feel, watching you eat that thing?"

Someone threw up across the room.

"Like that?" said Sebastian.

"I don't believe it. Milo's at it again."

Looking across the crowded cafeteria, the boys

made out Brian Hansen, Milo's only friend, brushing at his pants somewhat hysterically.

"You didn't have to do it all over my lunch!" Brian shrieked. "And look! Just look at my new sweater. My sister made me this sweater, Milo! What am I going to tell her? Milo! Milo, are you listening?"

Milo didn't hear Brian's tirade, nor did he hear the cheers and laughter, the stomping of feet and cries of "Attaboy, Milo! Way to go!" He didn't hear the monitor shout, "*Assez!* Enough!" nor recognize the voice as the French teacher's. He heard nothing but the sounds he himself made as he doubled over in pain. He thought he saw a hand reach out for him. He thought he heard someone say his name—for once, not unkindly. He collided with a chair. And then everything went black.

Milo Groot lay sprawled on the cafeteria floor, his cracked glasses inches away from his white face. The room fell silent, and remained so until Phil Greenburg, kneeling by the fallen boy's side, whispered, "Milo. *Mon Dieu.*"

7

"THE FLU," David said. He was leaning against a row of lockers, as Sebastian gathered his belongings after school.

"You're sure?"

David nodded. "I was in the office when Mrs. Kershaw called Milo's mother at work. I heard her say her son had thrown up at lunch and passed out and—"

"Yeah, yeah. I know that part."

"And that the school nurse said it looked like he still had a bug of some kind."

"A bug?" Sebastian asked, slamming his locker door shut and giving the combination lock a twirl.

"A bug, the flu, same thing."

"I wonder," said Sebastian.

David shook his head. "You're getting that look of yours," he said. "Listen, before you turn into Sherlock Holmes, we have to talk about today's show. We've got a fifteen-minute hole."

"What do you mean?"

"The beekeeper can't make it."

"Oh, great!" Sebastian dropped his books to the ground, and knelt down to tie his high-tops. "It's less than an hour till we tape, and the beekeeper lets us

[23]

know *now* he can't make it?" The shoelace broke in Sebastian's hand. "What about the guy from the animal shelter?"

"Oh, he's still coming."

"Well, I guess we can always do a half-hour with him. But we can't let him start talking about all the animals they put to sleep the way he did the last time he was on. My dad's really worried about the station's ratings. That's the last thing he needs."

Sebastian was attempting to knot his shoelace when he heard a girl's voice say, "Need some help?" He looked up to see Corrie and her two friends, Janis and Jennifer, standing over him. He returned Corrie's smile.

"You might say that," he said. Managing a crude knot, he stood up and explained about the fifteen-minute hole in his radio program.

"Oh, neat," Corrie said.

"Neat?"

"Listen, Sebastian, Janis and Jennifer are with me on this sports thing. We could come on your show and talk about girls playing football."

"We did that a couple of months ago, remember? I can't do the same show twice."

"But it wouldn't be the same show. This would be about my fight to make Pembroke Middle School allow girls on the football team. Just think, you'd have the principal's daughter taking my side against the school. You would go on Sebastian's show, wouldn't you, Jennifer?"

"Sure."

"I don't know," said Sebastian. "I'd have to clear it with my dad first. I don't want Mr. Hogan out for his blood like Harley is out for Milo's."

"You really think Harley is going to get Milo for what he wrote in the *Paragon*?" Janis asked.

"You never know what Harley will do. Listen, Corrie, I'll speak with my father today, and maybe we can work things out for next week. Okay?"

"That seems fair. You still have a problem, though."

"I know," said Sebastian. "A fifteen-minute hole and a guy who hot-wires puppies."

8 THE "THUNK-THUNK-THUNK" coming from behind Will Barth's closed door let Sebastian know at once that his father was not in the mood for talking. Whenever the station manager took to his dart board, it was a signal to everyone at WEB-FM that trouble was in the air.

"We can ask my dad about Corrie and the football show anytime," Sebastian said to David, "but I wish we could talk to him now about this week's show. We've only got twenty minutes till we tape. You're the writer. Any ideas?"

"I've got ten questions for you to ask the animal shelter guy. But that isn't going to fill a half-hour. Maybe we should talk to Uncle Harry."

Harry Dobbs, whose daily program, "A Few Raisins," had been on the air since before Sebastian's father was born, was everybody's "uncle," though no one knew if in fact he had any real family at all. When Will Barth had asked him once, he'd replied, "Why, Will, don't you know I have the largest family in the world, because everyone in the world is in it?" He was also fond of saying (and it was this that came to Sebastian's mind now), "I always have the time for any-one who has the time for an old fool like me."

"Good idea," Sebastian said. "Let's find Uncle Harry."

Before they had a chance to turn away, the thunking sound from inside Will's office stopped abruptly and was replaced by the voice of Harry Dobbs. Sebastian and David listened.

"It won't happen again, Will, I can promise you that," Harry said.

"Harry, I want to believe you, you know I do. But you've made promises before."

"And I've done my best to keep them. Will, I'm an old man—"

"And I'm a middle-aged man, growing older by the minute. I don't care how old you are, Harry. If it were up to me, you could keep on working here until you were a hundred and twenty. The point is, Herself hasn't given me a lot of options. The program is to be cancelled unless the ratings pick up. And the ratings aren't going to pick up unless some changes are made. Big changes."

"My gosh," Sebastian whispered. "I can't believe Dad is going to fire Uncle Harry."

"He can't," David said simply. "Firing Uncle Harry would be like bombing the Statue of Liberty. Hey, I've got it. Let's ask him to be on the show."

"Who?"

"Uncle Harry. He can fill our fifteen-minute hole talking about all his years with the radio station; you know, what it was like in the early days and all that. We'll get the listeners' sympathy for him."

"Not bad," Sebastian said. "It'll get us off the hook and help him at the same time. As soon as he comes out of Dad's office, we'll grab him.

"The thing is, from the sound of it, we've got more to worry about than just Uncle Harry. If Herself is thinking of cancelling his show because of ratings, what about ours? Last week, we did an exciting program on recycling soda cans; the week before that, how to get your parents to increase your allowance; the week before—"

"I get the picture," said David. "What we need is—"

"Controversy. Something hot. We need a *story*."

"How about Corrie's football thing?" David asked.

Sebastian nodded, but he was already thinking of something else. "There's a story at our school right now, and we've got a chance to scoop it. I have a hunch that someone's been poisoning Milo."

"Get real," David said.

"Where did his flu go?" Sebastian asked. "He seemed fine to me in shop class. Less than an hour later, he was sick again—*after* he'd eaten lunch."

"So why isn't anybody else saying it's poison? I

was in the office when the secretary called Milo's mother, Sebastian. Nobody's talking about food poisoning; they're saying he has a bug."

"I don't know. A cover-up, maybe?"

David snapped his fingers loudly. "You're right!" he practically shouted. "It's all a plot. Mr. Hogan is really a secret agent and—"

"You can make jokes if you like," Sebastian said, "but I'm going to get a scoop on a *real* story. You want to help?"

David sighed. "I know you too well not to trust your hunches," he said, "even when they sound as crazy as this one. Okay, count me in. What do I do?"

"You're my connection to the main office. Find out all you can about the cafeteria, where the food comes from, who does the ordering, and who's been in and out of the kitchen for the past few days."

"What does that leave for you to do?"

"Oh, I'll have plenty to do. You know how Miss Swille is always saying she can use more volunteers in the kitchen. Who better to help out than somebody whose mother owns a restaurant? First, though, you and I are going to visit a sick friend."

"I don't have any sick friends."

"Of course you do. Milo Groot."

"*Milo Groot?* Like I said, I don't have any sick friends, Sebastian. Except for you, maybe, and I've known you too long to tell anymore."

Just then, the boys saw the man from the animal shelter, Hiram Droner, coming down the hall in their direction. "What a week, what a week," he said as soon as he saw them. "We had to put two of the cutest little kittens to sleep. Just about broke my heart."

Sebastian and David exchanged looks, as the door to Will Barth's office opened. Sebastian's father and a defeated-looking Harry Dobbs walked through it.

"I thought I heard some familiar buzzing going on out here," Sebastian's father said.

"Hi, Dad."

"Hello, Uncle Will," David said. "Hi, Uncle Harry."

"Hello, lads," said Harry.

"Don't you boys have a show to tape?" Will asked.

"We were just waiting for Uncle Harry," said Sebastian.

"For me?" The color started to return to Harry's face.

"Sure. We need you, Uncle Harry."

"I'm glad to hear somebody does. What's up?"

"We've got a fifteen-minute hole," Sebastian explained. "Feel like being a guest on somebody else's show?"

Harry grabbed Sebastian's arm and marched him down the hall to the recording studio. "Did I ever tell you," he said, "about the time I interviewed Eleanor Roosevelt? Right here it was, in Studio B. A great lady, Eleanor Roosevelt, one of the greatest. And funny too. She told me a story . . ."

David turned to Hiram Droner. "Ready?"

"I will be," he replied, dabbing at his eyes. "I was just thinking about this German Shepherd. Nobody wanted him, you see. . . ."

David looked to Will Barth for sympathy, but the door had already closed. As he steered Hiram Droner down the hall, he could hear the "thunk-thunk-thunk" of a solitary dart game being resumed behind him.

9 HE PUSHED the doorbell and waited. After a second's silence, a chimed melody rang out. "Tchaikovsky," said Sebastian. Seeing David's questioning look, he added, "1812 Overture."

"You've been to Milo's house before?" David asked.

Sebastian shook his head. "It's one of my dad's favorite pieces of music, although I doubt he's ever heard it played on the doorbell. Do you think if I pushed it again that it would continue or repeat the phrase?"

"I don't know," said David, "but nobody's coming. Let's go."

"Nice try, coward," Sebastian said, pressing the doorbell. The refrain repeated itself. "Darn, I was hoping to hear the cannons. Now, that would have been something."

While they waited, David said, "Things worked out pretty well with Uncle Harry today, didn't they? I just wish your dad wasn't going to fire him."

"I talked to him about that," said Sebastian. "He isn't going to."

"Oh, good."

"He's not sure what to do, but he promised me he wouldn't do that. The problem is that nobody's into Uncle Harry's kind of show anymore. To make matters worse, the old guy rambles on a lot and forgets what he's talking about. Dad says it's gotten pretty bad lately; he doesn't know if it's age or what. But Herself called and said that Uncle Harry had better shape up or the show is going to be cancelled."

"It's weird."

"What is?"

"This lady nobody knows telling everybody what to do."

"She's rich and eccentric and she owns the radio station. Can't say it makes my dad's job any easier having an anonymous boss, but . . . wait a minute, I see somebody coming."

Milo's pale face replaced Sebastian's reflection, as the door slowly opened. "Barth. Lepinsky. What are you doing here?"

"I brought your homework," said Sebastian. "Can we come in? How are you feeling?"

"Lousy," Milo said, swinging the storm door open. "I'm not supposed to eat anything for twenty-four hours. Just drink water and weak tea. I'm not even supposed to be up, but nobody else is home. I'm kind of wobbly."

"So get back in bed," Sebastian said, looking at the art-covered walls of the Groot home. The place had the feeling of a museum or the waiting room of a high-priced dentist, he couldn't decide which. "I can explain the assignments to you in your room. Besides, there's something else I want to talk to you about."

"Follow me," said Milo, leading the way to the second floor.

If the living room was a museum, Milo's bedroom was a laboratory. Even before entering, Sebastian and David had an idea of what lay beyond the door adorned with the simple hand-lettered sign, "Resident Genius." The smell of mice permeated the entire upstairs. Where there weren't cages filled with the chattering, nibbling, wheel-running creatures, there were computer printouts and microscopes, petri dishes and globes (geographical, topographical and astrological), open books, closed books and notebooks. Nowhere on the walls were there posters of rock stars or movie stars; the only stars to be found in Milo's room belonged in constellations.

"Fun place," David whispered. "Remind me to see if it's booked for Christmas vacation."

Milo collapsed on his bed. "Homework can wait," he said. "You have my curiosity, Barth. What is this other matter you wish to discuss? My editorial, perhaps, and its ramifications?"

"Maybe," said Sebastian. "I don't know whether your editorial has anything to do with it, but I think you're being poisoned, Milo."

"Be serious," said Milo Groot.

"That's what *I* said." David was amazed to find himself agreeing with Milo about anything.

"Well, the most likely candidate is Harley," Milo went on. "And I would question his capability not only to conceive but to carry out such a crime."

"Look, Milo, Harley's been picking on you ever since first grade. He called you 'Four Eyes' then, and tripped you every time you walked past him, remember?"

Milo cringed. "Thank you for reminding me."

"Sorry," said Sebastian. "The point is—"

"The point is that Harley is a cretin. I know that. We all know that. We know too that Harley humiliated me in front of the entire school last spring at the awards assembly. But we also know that he didn't do anything any other student wouldn't have done if he'd had the opportunity. I am not exactly Mister Popularity at Pembroke Middle, Barth. If you want to compile a list of suspects for your poisoning caper, here's last year's yearbook. Open it to any page and point your finger."

Sebastian caught the book Milo tossed to him, and went on determinedly, "When you came to school today, how did you feel? You told me in shop class that the flu was gone. And you didn't look sick."

"I felt fine," said Milo. "So I have a strange virus. What of it?"

"When the nurse saw you, did she just take your

word for what was wrong with you?"

"That, and the evidence I left on the cafeteria floor."

"Have you seen a doctor yet?"

"My family doesn't use them. Well, we use them occasionally, but only for emergencies. You might say we're lapsed Christian Scientists." Milo stopped talking and fell back onto his pillow. Beads of sweat glistened on his forehead. "I think my fever's up again," he said, closing his eyes. "I'm tired. Can we talk about homework tomorrow, Barth?"

"Sure," said Sebastian, standing. David rose with him.

"Barth?"

"Yes?"

"You're serious, aren't you? You really do think someone's been poisoning me."

"I told you I did."

"In that case . . ."

"Yes?"

"In that case, may I join your investigation?"

Sebastian and David looked at each other in surprise.

"Please," Milo went on, his voice growing soft. "I can help. Look around you. I have spent a great deal of time investigating the mysteries of the universe in this little room of mine. I'm good at finding things out, Barth. Besides . . ." It seemed that sleep was about to overtake him. "Besides, if your theory is correct, I have a right to know who it is . . . who it is who hates me so much."

David knew what Sebastian's next words would be, even as he dreaded hearing them spoken.

"Consider yourself in, Milo."

Milo's eyes opened. "Really?"

"Really. Get some rest, okay? We'll be back tomorrow."

"Tomorrow," said Milo, shutting his eyes again. A few seconds later, he began to snore.

10

" 'FEARLESS,' " said Sebastian, reading the nameplate on the big stainless steel machine. "That's a funny name for a dishwasher."

Miss Swille laughed. "It is, isn't it?" she said. "They haven't made this kind for years. Why, she's even older than I am."

"We call her 'Fanny,' " said Barbara "Bea" Goode, one of the two assistant cooks.

This made Miss Swille laugh even harder. "Oh, Bea," she said, "you're not supposed to tell."

"Well, now, why not? If Sebastian is going to work in the kitchen, he'd better know what we mean when we talk about 'feeding Fanny.' Otherwise, we might get into hot water. So to speak."

Tears began to roll down Dorothy Swille's plump cheeks. "Bea Goode, you are such a *card*!"

"And that reminds me," Bea said to Sebastian. "As long as we're to be working together, it's no more 'Mrs. Goode' and 'Miss Swille.' I'm Bea and this here's Dottie." Nodding to the third member of the kitchen staff who, until this time had been silent, she added, "And Mrs. Dribowitz is Lill—"

"Mrs. Dribowitz," said Lillian Dribowitz, simultaneously picking up a cleaver and the rest of the sentence. She swung the cleaver down, neatly dissecting a head of lettuce. "I'm sorry," she said, looking up at Sebastian, "but I can't get used to students calling me by my Christian name. I just don't think it's proper. You're a nice boy, Sebastian, I know that. I'm sure you wouldn't abuse the privilege the way Eddie Davidson does, but—"

"*Harley* has problems," said Bea, holding an apron out to Sebastian. "Perhaps if you went easier with the boy, Lillian, he would have an easier time with you."

"I don't have no degree in social work, Bea," Lillian said. "And I'm not here to make friends with juvenile delinquents. I'm here to cook, not that anybody cares. We're out of mayonnaise."

"You know where it's kept," said Dottie Swille. The humor was gone from her voice; she was all business now. "Bea, will you get Sebastian started on the soup? Sixth grade will be here any minute."

Sebastian followed Bea to the stove, where a big vat of soup was boiling. "Apple chowder?" he cracked, hoping to make her laugh.

"What? Oh. No, it's minestrone. The apples are in the burgers." Sebastian had the feeling this was a conversation that would ordinarily have struck Bea Goode as funny. She was known for her sense of humor ("How could anybody called 'Bea Goode' *not* have a sense of humor?" she'd said). But she wasn't laughing now.

"Don't pay them any mind," she whispered to Sebastian, as she lifted the vat off the stove and onto a cart. "There's something going on between those two this year. It's Lillian, mostly. Maybe it's change of life. Oh, Sebastian, I shouldn't have said that. I mean . . . I don't know what I mean. She's plain nasty some days, and I don't get it."

Wheeling the cart to the food counter, Bea accepted Sebastian's offer of help in transferring the vat to its proper place. "Here come the hordes," she said.

"Bea," Dorothy Swille called out. "How is it? Does it need anything?" The cafeteria manager appeared suddenly, waving a plastic container in one hand, a large spoon in the other. "Let me taste it," she said. "Mm, it could use a little more." She held the container over the vat, tapping it lightly until its contents began to spill out into the soup.

"What's that?" Sebastian asked.

Miss Swille winked. "My secret herbs and spices," she said. "It's what makes my cooking special. My daddy used to say, 'Dottie, there's nobody cooks the way you do.'" She held the container against her heart and said, "He loved my cooking, my daddy did. Now I've got nobody to feed but me and nine cats."

"And four hundred *hungry* boys and girls," said Bea.

Suddenly, someone called out, "Hey, Sebastian,

are *you* working here now?" He recognized the voice as belonging to the sixth-grade wiseguy, Chris Buzzino.

"Soup?" Sebastian asked.

"I guess so," said Chris, taking a bowl. He looked at it and made a face. "Hey, it's got things floating in it. What kind of soup is this, anyway?"

"Cream of cootie," said Sebastian. "Next."

11 "HARLEY NEVER showed up," Sebastian told David later.

The two were holed up in the boys' room between classes. David had flipped open his pocket notebook to tell Sebastian what he had learned that morning. But Sebastian had spoken first.

"I know," David said. "He's absent."

"Sick?"

David shrugged. "Playing hooky probably. I heard Mrs. Kershaw say that Harley's been trying so hard to turn over a new leaf this year, he probably 'plumb wore out.' "

"Sounds like something Mrs. Kershaw would say. But what does she mean?"

"I'm not sure. Maybe his volunteering for cafeteria duty. That isn't exactly something you'd figure Harley to go in for, you know?" Sebastian nodded. "Speaking of cafeteria duty, how'd it go today?"

"Not bad. I didn't learn a whole lot." Sebastian took out a comb and began to run it through his hair. "Miss Swille and Mrs. Goode are really pretty nice, but Mrs. Dribowitz has a mean streak in her. And Bea, that's Mrs. Goode, she thinks there's something going on between her and Miss Swille."

"Oh, boy," said David. "Intrigue in the school cafeteria."

"Kitchen capers," Sebastian said, and both boys laughed. "What did you find out?"

"I wasn't sure what I was looking for, exactly. I asked a few questions, and learned that *a*, Miss Swille orders the food through a central office; *b*, she places an order once a week; *c*, some of the food comes from the government; *d*, she plans all the menus; *e*, all the cooking is done on the premises; and, *f*, I certainly am curious, aren't I. When I reached *f*, I decided I'd asked enough questions." David closed his notebook.

"Tomorrow," said Sebastian, "find out everybody who has access to the food—who's in and out of the cafeteria at all times of the day."

"You're in a better position to find that out than I am. Besides—" David's sentence was cut off by the boisterous arrival of Brad and Jason, a.k.a. Biker and Breeze.

"Geez, Biker," said Jason, ignoring Sebastian's and David's presence, "I thought you were gonna get killed, for sure."

"Did you see the look on Hogan's face? He thought it was a real tattoo." Sebastian noticed the red and blue snake winding its way up Brad's forearm. " 'Young man,' " Brad went on, imitating the principal, " 'do your parents know about this?' "

The two boys cracked up, as Brad removed a

pack of cigarettes from inside his notebook. He struck a match, and tossed the pack to Jason. "I dropped these in Greenburg's class the other day," he said. "I forgot to tell you."

"Did he see them?" Jason asked.

"I was so cool. I just said, 'Whoops.' Greenburg looked at me, but he didn't say anything."

"'Whoops'!" Jason cried.

They laughed even harder at this, mostly for the benefit of their unacknowledged audience, Sebastian was sure. He noticed that though they exhaled extravagantly, neither inhaled at all. As he nodded to David that it was perhaps time for them to leave, the door swung open and through it came Adam. The moment he saw Jason and Brad, he stiffened.

"Hi, Sebastian," he said. "Hi, David."

"Hi, Adam," both boys said.

Adam started to cough. "Kinda smoky in here, isn't it? Smells like a couple of stink bombs went off."

Sebastian saw Jason and Brad exchange looks. "Come on, bro," Brad whispered, loud enough for everyone to hear, "let's blow this pop stand." He crushed his cigarette beneath the heel of his shoe, and turned to leave. Jason immediately did likewise.

Adam rushed over to Brad and grabbed his arm. "Hey, hey," Brad said. "Back off, Adam. Be cool, my man."

"Stop it!" Adam shouted. "Stop talking like that."

"Talking like what? What's he getting at, Breeze?"

"You've got to learn to be cool, Adam," Jason said. "That's why we don't hang out with you anymore. You're not cool. Right, Biker?"

"Right, Breeze. Come on, let's go."

The door swung open and shut, and two-thirds of the Devil Riders were gone. The smell of their cigarette smoke lingered. When Adam turned back into the room, Sebastian started to speak. But Adam cut him off.

"Don't say anything," he said. His lower lip was bleeding. He must have bitten it, Sebastian thought. "Just leave me alone."

"If you want to come over after school..." Sebastian said.

"Leave me *alone*!" Adam shouted.

David tugged on his friend's sleeve. "I think he's trying to tell us something," he said.

"Right," said Sebastian, picking up his books. "Right."

12

THIS TIME, Milo's mother came to the door.

"You must be Barth and Lepinsky," she said, briskly ushering them into the house. "I'm Cecily Groot. Milo has told me so much about you. I'm certainly pleased that he's found friends other than that Hansen boy. Don't misunderstand me, Brian comes from a good family, but I do wonder about his influence on Milo sometimes." David started to giggle, thinking of Brian Hansen as someone a mother would worry about. "Are you known as anything but Barth and Lepinsky, by the way? Please call me Cecily."

"I'm Sebastian."

"And I'm David."

"Sebastian. David. Oh! Sebastian."

"Yes?"

"Is your mother Katie Hallem?"

Sebastian nodded.

"I've heard her talk about her son, Sebastian. But I didn't make the connection because Milo calls you Barth. And of course your mother's last name is different from yours. How liberated of her. I adore her little restaurant. She sells my elderberry jam there. Do you know my elderberry jam? You don't? I make it from my own tree, right here in the yard. Well, you go up and see Milo, I know how he's looking forward to your visit. He's desperate about missing school. School is his entire *raison d'être*. When you come down, I'll serve you some biscuits and jam. Would you like that?"

"Well . . ." David said.

"That would be very nice," said Sebastian. "How is Milo, anyway?"

"Much improved, thank you. I expect he'll be able to go back tomorrow."

"I thought he was going to be out a whole week. His flu—"

"Flu? He doesn't have the flu. He ate something, that's all. Besides, there's no such thing as flu. It's an illusion. Now, you two run along, and I'll brew some tea."

"Translation," David whispered, climbing the stairs. "*Raison d'être*: reason for being."

"Thank you," said Sebastian. "Now translate his mother."

13

AS PREDICTED, Milo Groot returned to school the following day. Harley was back too, wearing a worried expression and the same clothing he'd last been seen in. Both appeared first thing that morning in the principal's office.

"Milo," David later reported to Sebastian between classes, "came in demanding that Mr. Hogan consider his editorial and do something about the quote rampaging marauders in leather jackets unquote."

"What did Mr. Hogan say to that?"

"He told Milo that he'd received no reports of rampaging, and that there was nothing inherently evil about leather jackets."

"Did he then tell Milo to put that in his pipe and smoke it?"

"No, but he thanked Milo for sharing his thoughts on the matter, and told him his opinions were welcome anytime. Milo left in a huff."

"'In a huff'?" said Sebastian. "Where'd you come up with that?"

"Mrs. Kershaw. I'm only telling you what I heard

Mrs. Kershaw and Mr. Hogan talking about later. I wasn't there for the main event."

"What about Harley? Did they mention him?"

"Yep. Harley was called in to explain his absence."

"His mother didn't send a note?"

"He doesn't have a mother."

"I thought he did."

"Everybody thinks that, because that's what Harley says. But this morning, he wasn't talking. Mr. Hogan said he's going to call the family's social worker.

"Oh, oh, here comes your friend Milo. Does he have to be in on our investigation, Sebastian? I don't think I can stand the smell of mice much longer. I think one of them died in there yesterday."

"Barth. Lepinsky." Milo extended a clipboard in their direction. "How about signing my petition?" he said. "I'm demanding that Mr. Hogan do something about the Devil Riders."

"Sorry," said Sebastian. "I signed Corrie's football petition this morning. I believe in harrassing the principal on only one issue at a time. Besides, I'm late for lunch duty. Which reminds me, David, did you find out who has access to the cafeteria?"

"How much do you want for one day?" David said. "I'll see what I can find out tomorrow." A bell rang loudly. "Now I'm late. See you, Sebastian."

"See you."

"But, Barth," said Milo Groot.

"See you, Milo."

Sebastian started toward the hall leading to the cafeteria. At the corner, Harley, Jason and Brad stood gaping at an open magazine and jabbing each other as each page was turned. Sebastian couldn't help wondering again what made Jason and Brad want to be Harley's friends, to wear fake tattoos and smoke cigarettes, to huddle in hallways and act all excited over pictures of motorcycles.

He wasn't sure it was the right thing to do, but he turned back to Milo and called out, "Hey, Groot!"

"Yes, Barth?"

"Wait up. I'll sign your petition."

14

BEFORE SEBASTIAN had come to work in the kitchen, he'd always been impressed by the air of camaraderie that seemed to exist in the world beyond the lunch line. Dottie Swille and Bea Goode were hearty laughers; even Lillian Dribowitz was good for a chuckle now and then. But today the air held the chill of unspoken resentments and petty angers. Lillian kept "throwing darts Dottie's way," as Bea put it in a whisper to Sebastian. And both Dottie and Harley seemed burdened by private troubles.

Sebastian was struck by the difference in the Harley who was now grating cheese, eyes downcast, lips moving to some secret litany, and the one he'd seen not five minutes earlier out in the hall. There was something about the boy that was beginning to fascinate him.

He noticed Dottie shake her head. She was doing that a lot today. She seemed to be having a conversation with herself, and she didn't appear to like what she heard herself saying. Bea shook her head from time to time too, but that was in response to Dottie's silence and Lillian's darts.

He was glad when the eighth-graders arrived for lunch. At least he could make jokes with his friends about the apple croquettes. And when he'd finished serving, he could observe the lunch-time scene. He smiled to see both Corrie and Milo circulating around the crowded room with their petitions, vying with each other for signatures. Corrie, he noticed, was having greater success.

He didn't remember if Milo had bought lunch, or brought one with him. Perhaps he was so busy trying to get signatures that he wasn't planning to eat at all. Sebastian was mildly disappointed to think that Milo might not eat and would therefore not be throwing up. He couldn't believe he felt such a thing; at the same time, he couldn't deny that he was hungry for clues, eager for substantiation that his poisoning theory was correct. He found himself watching Milo's face for a change of color. Far from growing pale, Milo's cheeks were growing ruddier as the pitch of his anti-gang crusade grew more and more vehement.

All at once, he saw Jason and Brad start across the room toward Milo. The cafeteria monitor saw them too, and took a warning step forward. The buzz of conversation dwindled. Everything grew still. Milo's cheeks lost some of their color, but he stood his ground.

"Boys," the monitor said.

That was as far as it got. Just then, at a table in the corner, Justin Greer threw up. The room exploded with cheers and groans. The noise was so great no one noticed at first that Lindsay Carmichael was throwing up, too.

But Sebastian noticed. So did Bea Goode. "Mercy," she said, "maybe it's all the apples." They both turned to Dottie Swille, who didn't say a word. She just shook her head.

15

THERE WASN'T much talk about rampaging gangs or girls playing football the rest of that Friday afternoon. Instead, Pembroke Middle School was buzzing with speculation about the mysterious illness attacking its students. Sebastian was no longer alone in espousing poisoning as the cause, although there was some debate as to whether the poisoning was intentional or accidental. Walking home with Corrie and David, Sebastian made it clear where he stood.

"Miss Swille," he said, "has been with the school twenty-five years. In all that time, whatever may have been said about her cooking, there hasn't been one health code violation against her. She's always run a clean kitchen, and I don't see any reason to think she isn't doing so now."

"So?" said David.

"How do you know all this?" Corrie asked.

"She told me herself. I know, I know what you're thinking. Self-protection. I don't think so. I don't think she'd lie about it. She was really shocked when Justin and Lindsay got sick today. She practically started to cry."

"I repeat," David said. "So?"

"So I don't think the poisoning was accidental. The question is—"

"The question is," said David, adjusting his backpack, "why are you so convinced it's poisoning when the school administration says it's flu?"

"Wrong," Sebastian replied. "The question is, why is the school administration lying?"

"Oh, come on."

"Really, Sebastian," said Corrie, "I don't see how they could get away with lying. Or why they would bother in the first place."

"I don't know, I don't know. Maybe they have something—or somebody—to protect."

"I was in the office after eighth-grade lunch today," David said. "I was there when the report came from the nurse's office. I was there when Miss Swille came in and called her boss, who called the Board of Health, who came right over and investigated."

"They haven't finished their investigation," Sebastian said. "I talked with Miss Swille after sixth period. She told me they came and took samples of everything served for lunch today and that they won't have the results until Monday. The verdict isn't in."

"Did she say anything else?"

"Only that she was worried," said Sebastian.

"About what?"

"About the findings of the Board of Health. She said to me, 'I can't have a blemish on my record, Sebastian. Not now. Not after twenty-five years.' Then she got real quiet, and I left her alone."

"What if somebody is out to get her?" Corrie suggested. Sebastian looked at her. "You know, to frame her or something?"

David laughed. "Sure. Somebody's still got it in for her for the tunafish dreamboats. What I say is, if it *is* poisoning, then what if *she's* the one who's out to get somebody? Or everybody? Hey, maybe she wants to wipe out the whole student body."

Sebastian recalled Adam's joking about Miss Swille's hating kids. But that was impossible; she *liked* kids. Didn't she?

"Come on, Sebastian," David said, "get that look off your face. You'll see. It's the flu, nothing more than the flu."

16

THAT NIGHT at dinner, Sebastian discussed the matter with his mother and grandmother. His father was at the table too, but his attention seemed to be on problems of his own.

"Poisoning can occur for all sorts of innocent reasons," Katie said, helping herself to some brown rice. "If food isn't served at just the right temperature, for instance, or hasn't been refrigerated. Some foods are particularly troublesome—fish, chicken, mayonnaise."

"Mayonnaise?"

Katie nodded. "Mayonnaise, if it's been left out, can turn bad and cause salmonella poisoning."

Sebastian looked down at his poached salmon, and Katie laughed.

"There's no relationship between salmonella poisoning and salmon," she said. "Relax."

"What's it like?"

"Salmonella poisoning? Chills, vomiting, diarrhea—"

"Really, you two," Jessica Hallem said at last. "Is the dinner table the place for this discussion?"

"Perhaps not, Mother," said Katie. "But it *is* disturbing to think that students are being poisoned at Sebastian's school."

"Fiddle-faddle," Jessica said. "Sebastian himself said that the official word is influenza. The fact that the symptoms showed themselves in the cafeteria is coincidence, surely."

"It's a possible coincidence, I admit," said Sebastian's mother, "but an unlikely one. The thing that troubles me is Dottie Swille's reputation."

"As what?" Jessica snorted. "An eccentric? She's a pathetic soul, living alone with her twenty cats—"

"Nine," said Sebastian.

"Cats are lovely pets," Jessica said, with a downward nod to the black one curled around her left foot, "but they do not replace human companionship. Oh, I don't mean to be unkind, but what does anyone really know about poor Dorothy Swille?"

"I know that she cares about the children in her school," Katie replied forcefully. "I know that she worries about nutrition and good health. Yes, she's a bit of an eccentric. She must be to come up with some of the concoctions she does. But apple chili dogs aren't going to harm anyone."

"Good heavens," said Jessica Hallem, "does she really serve such things?"

"And apple lasagna," Sebastian said, laughing, "and apple burgers. Hey, Mom, is there anything poisonous in apples?"

"Not that I know of. Maybe, with all the apples she's been serving, it's just been a case of too much of a good thing."

"What is it they used to say about Dorothy Swille?" Jessica said, more to herself than anyone else.

The phone rang, and Sebastian jumped up to get it. "It's Corrie. Can I go over to her house for a while?"

"*May* I," said Jessica.

Katie said, "Sure. How about loading the dishwasher first?"

Turning back to the phone, Sebastian said, "I'll see you soon."

Alone in the kitchen a few minutes later, Sebastian thought about what his mother had said. If Miss Swille really cared about the children in her school, and he believed she did, how could she have poisoned them, even accidentally? If she was so careful about nutrition, wouldn't she have noticed something was wrong before it was too late? Or was there more to her than most people knew, as his grandmother had suggested? Perhaps all those years of living with only cats for company had affected her mind.

Maybe his mother was rallying to her cause because she was in the food business herself and knew that the same thing could happen to her. Or maybe she knew something about Miss Swille she wasn't saying. The possibility that she just might be sympathetic to another human being in trouble didn't occur to him then, though it did a moment later when he heard her voice from the next room.

"Oh, Will," she was saying to Sebastian's father, "I'm so sorry. How will you tell him?"

"I don't know. What *can* I say? How can I make him understand?"

"It's so unfair. She acts like some sort of Greek goddess on high, just pulling strings and making people do what she tells them to do. It's never been this bad, though."

"It's never been this bad because the ratings have never been this bad."

"But to cancel his show . . ."

Sebastian felt his stomach tighten. Were they talking about Uncle Harry or about him? And which would hurt worse?

He was trying to decide whether to go in and confront his father, when Jessica entered the kitchen and said, "I've remembered."

"Remembered what, Gram?"

"What they used to say about Dottie Swille. 'Higgledy-piggledy Dorothy Swille, never married and never will.' "

Sebastian frowned. "She's a nice lady," he said. "Why do they need to say things like that?"

"Oh, you know how people are," said Jessica. "One hurt is born of another. Until we stop feeling pain, we'll be unable to stop spreading it."

17

TWENTY MINUTES LATER, Sebastian was sitting on the worn leather hassock in Corrie's living room, as the Wingate family whizzed by him like commuter trains at rush hour. Only the basset hound stayed long enough to keep Sebastian company, and that, Sebastian suspected, was probably because no one else was paying attention to him. When he found himself alone with the dog, he reached down and scratched him behind the ears.

"Poor Roger," he said, "nobody loves you." Roger dropped the short distance to the ground and rolled over on his back. "You don't even mind, do you? As long as there's somebody around to feed you and rub your tummy, what do you care about love, right?"

"Don't be silly, Sebastian," said Corrie's mother, trying to fasten a strand of pearls and search for a lost shoe at the same time. "Roger needs love as much as you or I. And he gets plenty of it around here, believe me. You're spoiled, aren't you, boy? Isn't that the truth?"

"Why does he always look so sad then?"

"He's sad," said Ginny Wingate, "because he hid my shoe and can't remember where it is."

"Let's not blame the dog, dear," Corrie's father said, coming down the stairs. He was picking at a spot on his tie. "What *is* this, anyway? Oh, hello, Sebastian. Been here long?"

"About five minutes, Reverend Wingate. How are you?"

"Found it," said Corrie's mother, retrieving her shoe from under a bookcase.

"Any teeth marks?"

"Not a one. I forgive you, Roger."

"You can't forgive someone," said Junior Wingate, "for a trespass uncommitted. What *is* this stain?"

Ginny squinted at her husband's chest. "Dog slobber," she said, as a timer sounded in the kitchen. "Corrie! The spaghetti!"

Her husband eyed the prone basset hound reproachfully. "Roger," he intoned, in his God-at-Sinai voice.

Roger whimpered.

"Reverend Wingate," said Sebastian, "may I ask you a question?"

"Of course, Sebastian, I always have time for a question."

"The problem is, you may not have time for the answer," Ginny said. "We're five minutes late for the Siddonses' as it is."

"Never mind," Sebastian said, "I can ask you another time. It's kind of, well, kind of a question of theology, I suppose."

"Oh, my. Please ask."

"Do you think that one hurt is born of another?"

"Oh, my," Junior Wingate said again.

"That's what my grandmother says. She says that people hurt each other because they've been hurt themselves. Do you think that's true? And, if it is, then how do we ever stop hurting each other?"

Corrie's father continued to pick at his tie. "That's a good question," he said. "If we consider the words of Saint Paul in Romans, chapter twelve, verse twenty-one—"

"Sebastian doesn't want to hear scripture," said his wife, returning from the kitchen. "Corrie, please come down here and finish fixing your brothers' dinner. And tell your sister if she wants a ride with us, she'd better hurry. Dear, I'm sorry, I can't get these pearls, will you try? I don't mean to rush you, but we don't have time for scriptures. Tell Sebastian what *you* think. That's what matters."

"Scriptures would take less time," said Reverend Wingate, fussing clumsily at the back of his wife's neck. "Sebastian, your question deserves more than a hurried response. I will give it thought, I promise you. But I can say this. There is no way for people to stop hurting one another except to *stop*. Take the arms race."

"Oh, dear," said Ginny, glancing at her watch.

"If we justify building up our own arsenals because *they* have more weapons, then we only heap one folly on top of another. There comes a time when we must say, 'Enough! I don't have to have more toys than you. I don't need the last word. I will turn the other cheek.' "

"Mom!" Buster Wingate screamed from the top of the stairs. "Drew hit me!"

"Turn the other cheek," Ginny shouted back. "Let's go, Junior. Thanks for helping Corrie babysit, Sebastian. Good luck. You'll need it—even more than theology."

18

AS THE NEXT DAY was Saturday, Sebastian and David were able to pay an early visit to Milo Groot.

"You should have seen the spaghetti war at Corrie's house last night," Sebastian said, as the two boys waited at the front door.

"Spaghetti war?"

"Yeah. Buster was still mad at Drew for hitting him. When I suggested to him at the dinner table that he turn the other cheek, he took me literally. Drew got him with a meatball."

"Kids," said David. "How much of a mess did they make?"

"A big one. It didn't take long to clean up, though. We had the help of an expert cleaner-upper."

"Corrie?"

"Roger."

Suddenly, Milo appeared. "I thought you guys would never get here," he said. "I've got news. Follow me."

"P.U.," said David, when they'd closed the door to Milo's room. "I hate to tell you this, Milo, but as Hiram Droner would say, it smells like death in here."

"That's because one of my mice died."

"Just what I thought. Have you thought of disposing of the body?"

"I have," said Milo. "It's just that I didn't discover it right away. I was sick, remember? Anyway, I don't want to talk about that. She was my favorite mouse. There'll never be another one like Fritzie."

"At least not another one who *smells* like her," said David.

"What's your news?" Sebastian said.

"Well, Barth, it isn't news exactly. More like speculation. Still, it is interesting. You see, I agree with you that these poisonings are deliberate. If so, I asked myself, who would be out to poison me, Justin Greer and Lindsay Carmichael? What's the connection between the three of us? We're not friends, we're not even in the same homeroom. So what do we have in common?"

"And?"

Milo began to pick his nose, a habit Sebastian attributed to his being only ten, though he could remember himself being broken of it long before that age. Perhaps, he mused, geniuses didn't concern themselves about such mundane things as appearances.

"*And,*" said Milo, wiping his finger on his shirt-sleeve, "there is only a connection if you look at the three of *us* vis-a-vis the three of *them.*"

"Us?" said David. "Them?"

"The three victims," Milo replied. "And the three Devil Riders."

"I should have known you'd find a way to bring them into it," David said.

"Listen. Listen to me, Lepinsky. Everyone knows that Harley hates me. Okay, I said I didn't think he had the brains to think this thing up, or to pull it off. But he isn't alone anymore, is he? Now he has two brainy friends, Jason and Brad. Well, brainy is a relative term, but relative to Harley a *maggot* is brainy."

"Nice image," David muttered, "in light of the odor in here."

"Now, it so happens," Milo went on excitedly, "that Justin Greer and Brad West are next-door neighbors. And Lindsay Carmichael and Jason Bruxter—"

"Let me guess," David said. "They had the same piano teacher in the third grade, right?"

"Better than that. They're cousins!" Milo pounded the fist of one hand into the palm of the other, and waited for a response.

"So?" said Sebastian.

"So there's a connection."

"There's a connection between every one of us," Sebastian said. "We're all students in the same school, we live in the same town, we might be in Sunday school class together or have the same dentist."

"But neighbors and cousins," Milo persisted,

"are much stronger relationships than fellow students or dental patients."

"I don't know, maybe there is something to your theory. I just wonder if we're not looking too hard for a connection. After all, the poisonings could be random, you know."

"You mean I was a victim by chance? *Twice*?"

"It's possible."

"Unlikely."

"But possible."

"Why would someone be poisoning the eighth grade at random? What's to be gained?"

"That," Sebastian said, "is just one of the questions left to be answered."

19

"HEY, ADAM."

"Hey, Sebastian."

The two boys brushed shoulders before Sebastian took in the change in his classmate's Monday morning appearance. "Adam," he cried out, "where'd you get the shiner?"

Adam continued down the hall. "My sister," he said over his shoulder.

Sebastian entered the school office. "Did you see what Joanna did to Adam?" he asked David, who was busy stapling. David put his fingers to his lips, nodding toward Mr. Hogan's closed door.

"Hi, Mrs. Kershaw," Sebastian said softly to the secretary.

"Hello, Sebastian. What can we do for you?"

"Nothing. I was just looking for David."

"It looks like you've found him," said Sandy Kershaw, with an almost-relaxed smile. "Do you have a few minutes? I'm sure he could use some help getting those reports stapled." A buzzer sounded. "Oh, dear," she said, looking toward the room the students called the "twilight zone," "I hope Mr. Hogan isn't going to be too hard on those two. I don't know what's gotten into them." As she opened the door, Sebastian caught a glimpse of Jason and Brad standing slump-shouldered and sullen before the principal's desk.

"I was trying to hear what was going on in there," David confided, once they were alone. "Adam's sister didn't give him that black eye. Jason and Brad did. The three of them got caught fighting five minutes ago."

"What about?"

"That's what I was trying to hear."

"Was Harley involved?"

David shook his head. "Nowhere in sight. And speaking of Harley, Sebastian, he wasn't involved in any poisoning either."

"The report came in from the Board of Health?"

"Right. No poisoning."

"No poisoning?"

"No poisoning. The flu."

"But Justin and Lindsay are back in school already," Sebastian said.

"A twenty-four hour bug," said David. "Just like Milo's. And don't tell me it's a cover-up."

"You have such faith in the administration," said Sebastian. "An administration, I might add, that just may be trying to hide a scandal."

"You're right," David said, hitting the stapler, "I have more faith in an administration that *may* be hiding a scandal than I do in a reporter who's looking for one."

"What's that supposed to mean?"

"You know what it means. You're looking for a scoop, Sebastian. You're not seeing straight. Mr. Hogan is an honest person. He wouldn't cover something up or play favorites or any of that stuff."

Just then, the door to the principal's office opened. "Next time, boys," Mr. Hogan was saying, "I'll have to telephone your parents. Remember that."

"Yes, sir," said Jason Bruxter.

"Right," Brad West mumbled.

Sebastian and David heard the two boys start to giggle as soon as they'd reached the outside hall.

"I hope I wasn't too lenient," Mr. Hogan said to his secretary. "I'd have called Jason's father *this* time if it weren't for that school board election coming up."

"I understand, Hap," said Sandy Kershaw. "Dan Bruxter's probably going to be the next president and you don't want to get off on the wrong foot with him. There's nothing wrong with keeping quiet at times. That's just politics."

David's hand was poised over the stapler, as he and Sebastian exchanged a look.

20

THE TWO MET at Sebastian's locker later that morning. "It's useless," David said.

"What is?"

"*Anybody* can get into the kitchen. There's the cafeteria staff. And the volunteers. And the delivery men."

"How many is that?" Sebastian asked, closing his locker door. "Fifteen, twenty at most?"

"The teachers come and go whenever they want. They do it a lot, Sebastian, especially on days when Miss Swille bakes cookies. And then there are the runners."

"Oh, yeah, the runners."

"Every morning, somebody from every class goes to the cafeteria with the hot lunch order. And it's a different somebody every day. Practically everybody in my class has been a runner at one time or another."

Sebastian frowned. "That does complicate matters," he said.

"I'd say it does more than that," said David.

"Well, thanks for trying. Any word on Mr. Hogan?"

"Yeah, I heard him speaking in code on the phone."

"You still don't believe me, do you?"

"When I'm with you, I do. But when I have a little time to think about it, I'm not so sure."

"There's your problem," said Sebastian. "You think too much." The bell rang, and the two boys sprinted in opposite directions, David about to be late for his math class, Sebastian for cafeteria duty.

If Sebastian was in fact late, Dottie Swille didn't seem to notice or to care. She was already at the counter, ladling out apple noodle soup and words of advice. "Eat your broccoli, dear," she said, smiling. "It's high in Vitamin A." Behind her, Bea Goode and Harley Davidson transported trays while loudly dueling their favorite songs by Willie Nelson and Bruce Springsteen.

Standing at the sink, his hands under the hot, running water, Sebastian closed his eyes and listened. This was the cafeteria the way he'd imagined it to be: Miss Swille cooing like a contented pigeon, the clatter of silverware and the banging of trays, the chatter of students, the singing of the kitchen staff. Maybe he'd gotten carried away with this poison thing, after all. He wasn't ready to believe it was the flu, but perhaps the poisoning was accidental. His ears heard only harmony now, only harmony until—

"Does this look like thirty-five cents to you? Don't

you try to shortchange me, young man. Hey, hey, where are you going?"

Sebastian's eyes snapped open. Lillian Dribowitz was standing beside the cash register, her arm outstretched, her eyes flaring angrily. "Miss Swille," she called, without looking away from the object of her anger, "Miss Swille, will you please call Mr. Hogan's office?"

"What's the problem, Lillian?" Dottie asked.

Sebastian saw the cashier's shoulders rise a fraction of an inch, probably in response to being called by her first name in front of students. "The problem," she said, turning sharply to address the cafeteria manager, "is that Darryl Johnson thinks he can pay thirty cents for an orange when he knows it costs thirty-five cents."

Dottie Swille continued ladling her soup. "Let's not make a fuss over five cents, Lillian." She turned and added quietly, so that the students in line wouldn't hear, "I'd rather see Darryl Johnson pay what he can for a piece of fruit than go without or snitch it when we're not looking."

Lillian Dribowitz slammed the cash register drawer shut. "I didn't know we were a welfare agency now," she said tightly. "I'm going on my break."

"But, Lillian—"

"I'm entitled," said Lillian Dribowitz, storming out of the kitchen. "And don't come looking for me. I'll be back when I'm good and ready."

Dottie Swille took a deep breath. "Sebastian," she said, "would you take over here, please?" She grabbed a pillow from under the counter to place on the cash register stool (she was a good head shorter than Lillian Dribowitz), and apologized to the student who was waiting in line. "Sorry, Melanie," she said. "Even grown-ups fight from time to time."

"Tell me about it," the girl named Melanie replied. "My mom's been married four times."

Dottie gave a startled laugh and turned to Sebastian. "Nothing's going to get me down today," she told him. "Do you know why?"

"I can guess," Sebastian said.

"There isn't an ounce of suspicion left," she said. "My kitchen—and my apples—received a clean bill of health, across the board. I'll tell you, Sebastian, when Bea said it could have been the apples, I just about died."

"Why?" Sebastian asked, putting down the ladle. "Do apples go bad or something?"

Waiting for the last student to pick up her tray and move away, Dottie Swille leaned against the cash register, and said, "It isn't that they go bad. But the seeds are poisonous."

Bea and Harley stopped their singing to listen.

"Apple seeds contain prussic acid," Dottie explained. "Also known as cyanide."

Sebastian whistled through his teeth.

"Could they kill you?" Harley asked. Sebastian

turned and noticed for the first time that Harley wasn't wearing his usual motorcycle outfit. In fact, the plaid button-down shirt looked new.

"Only if you were to eat a great many," said Dottie. "It seemed awful far-fetched to me. I mean, first, the seeds would have had to get into the cooking. And, second, as I say, it would have taken a lot of them. Still, I've been using a lot lately—"

"It's a government program," Bea told the boys. "October is apple month. We're getting so many surplus apples that if we don't use them, they'll rot."

"Lucky I'm such a creative cook," Dottie Swille remarked. "Oh, boys, if that report had come in saying my kitchen was the cause of those children getting sick, it would have ruined *everything*. Not to mention, of course, how bad I would have felt."

"What do you mean, it would have ruined everything?" Sebastian asked.

Miss Swille exchanged a glance with Bea Goode. "I can't really talk about it because I'm not supposed to know," she said. "Let's just say that my twenty-five years here are not going to go unmarked."

There was a loud bang. Lillian Dribowitz had returned to the kitchen and dropped a tray of silverware into the sink.

"Time to feed Fanny," Bea commented.

"I'll do it," said Harley.

"Why, thank you, Harlan," Miss Swille said. "Some days it's a positive delight having you around."

Harley smiled, not even bothering to correct his name.

Sebastian understood the change in her; what, he wondered, accounted for the change in Harley?

21

"HOW SHOULD I KNOW?" Adam said. The dark glasses he wore to cover his black eye made it hard to read his face.

"I just thought," said Sebastian, "that Jason and Brad might have told you something about Harley."

Adam shifted uncomfortably in his seat. He glanced at the clock: one minute until the bell would ring for French class. He glanced at the door: there was no sign of the teacher. "I have nothing to say to those creeps," he said. "And they have nothing to say to me."

"Then how'd the fight start this morning? Somebody must have said something to somebody."

"Not much. I told them I thought they were kidding themselves, that's all. I said, 'One of these days, you guys are going to get bored being Harley's clones, and when you change back into who you really are—'"

"Which is what?" Sebastian said.

"Which is a couple of spoiled little rich kids from Riverview Estates, that's what. When they drop Harley, they're going to be real, real sorry—because Harley isn't going to like it. And they're going to find that their old friends aren't interested anymore."

"Old friends like you, huh?"

Adam looked up to the clock. Five seconds.

"Right," he said.

The bell rang, and Phil Greenburg swept into the room.

"*Alors, mes enfants*," he said, turning into Monsieur Hameauvert, "*nos histoires*. Who has written a story they'd like to read?"

Harley Davidson raised his hand.

22

"WHAT DO I KNOW about Harley?" said David, repeating Sebastian's question. The two friends had stopped for some pizza on the way home from school. "That he's an obnoxious bully who gets in trouble on the average of three times a week; that he likes picking on anybody smaller or smarter than he is, especially Milo Groot who is both; that he's a wiseguy and a show-off; that he likes motorcycles, and dresses as if he's just been in an accident with one—"

"Not today," said Sebastian. "Today he was wearing new clothes. Button-down shirt. Chinos. Hush Puppies."

"Hush Puppies? I don't believe it."

"What else do we know about him? What do you know about him from working in the school office?"

"I know he's Mr. Hogan's most frequent visitor."

"Seriously."

"I'm being serious. All right. He lives in that big stone house up off Route 7. The one with the red mailbox out front."

"Nice place," said Sebastian, wiping tomato sauce from his chin.

"It's his grandfather's, I guess. He lives there with the old man, his father and two sisters. I don't know what the story is on his mother except that she isn't around. His father works at the Mobil station on Main Street. He owns the place, I think. That's what Harley says. The family has a social worker, I don't know why. And that's all I know."

"Not a lot."

"What do *you* know?"

"Less. I wish we knew more."

"Don't tell me we're going to become Harley's friends now too," said David, catching a glob of dripping cheese with his tongue.

"I don't think we could be Harley's friends if we wanted to. But I have a hunch—"

"Oh, oh."

"—that whatever happens, Harley's going to get the blame. I just wish I knew if he deserves it."

"He deserves it, he deserves it."

"Guilty until proven innocent?" Sebastian asked.

"Why not?" David said. He's always been a troublemaker, right? So, when there's trouble . . ."

"Blame it on Harley."

Nodding, David said, "You want to share another slice of pizza?"

"Sure. It's pretty good today. Just one thing it could use, though."

"What's that?"

"Apples."

23

OF ONE HUNDRED and ten students in the eighth grade at Pembroke Middle School, seventy-seven threw up at lunch the following day. Of those seventy-seven, two fainted. And one of those two was hospitalized.

Milo and Adam were among the afflicted, while Jason, Brad and Sebastian went unscathed. Jason and Brad had brought lunches from home; Sebastian was simply living up to his reputation as "the boy with the iron stomach."

School was immediately cancelled for the rest of the day, as parents were summoned to retrieve their ailing children. Miss Swille was told to report to the Department of Food Services at once. And the Board of Health shut down the cafeteria until further notice.

In all the commotion, no one noticed Harley Davidson empty his locker and walk out the front door.

24

THERE WAS NO ONE home to greet Sebastian when he arrived early from school but his two cats, Boo and Chopped Liver, and theirs was less a greeting than a scornful acknowledgement that their afternoon naps had been rudely disturbed. Glad to be alone, Sebastian dropped his bookbag on the kitchen table and went to the refrigerator to pour himself a glass of milk.

As he sat down, his eyes fell on the large lump in his bookbag. What had made him do it? he wondered. Why had he taken it? He'd been following a hunch, sure, but he'd also tampered with evidence. And if his hunch turned out to be correct, he was not only tampering with evidence, he was concealing it. There was a part of him, the part that liked Miss Swille, that hoped his hunch was wrong. But another part, the part that wanted the truth (or a scoop, he wasn't sure which), that hoped he was right. He was about to open the bookbag when the telephone rang.

"I concede," said the voice on the other end. "It was poison, not the flu."

"It doesn't take much to convince you. Just seventy-seven kids throwing up in unison."

"That must have been quite a sight," David said. "Like Niagara Falls."

Sebastian laughed. "It really isn't funny, you know. Justin Greer's in the hospital."

"I know. Hey, you want to come over?"

"Not right now."

"I could come over there."

"I don't think so. Can I call you back later?"

"Sebastian, are you having one of your moods?"

"What are you talking about?"

"You know what I'm talking about. First, you don't want to hang out, now you don't want to talk. You have these moods, you know, where you get all quiet and mysterious."

"I do?"

"Yeah. Look, don't worry about it. You can call me when you're back to normal, whatever that is. I'll be here."

"Thanks."

"Sure. What are friends for?"

Sebastian replaced the receiver and thought: Quiet and mysterious. That's just the way the cafeteria manager acted right before all those kids got sick.

He opened the bookbag and removed a plastic container. He shook it, wondering what exactly were Dorothy Swille's secret herbs and spices.

25

FIFTEEN MINUTES LATER, Sebastian poured a small amount of the mixture into an envelope, then hid the plastic container with the remaining herbs and spices in his sock drawer. Next, he called David and told him to meet him in front of his house at once. When David commented on this rather sudden return to normalcy, Sebastian replied, "The time for thinking is over. Now we've got to act."

"You know," David said, joining his friend on the sidewalk, "there *are* other people investigating this thing—like the school administration, the Department of Food Services, the Board of Health, the police department. I don't know what you think you're going to find that they aren't."

"Probably nothing. It's just a question of who finds something *first*. Did you say the police are involved?"

"Yeah. My dad just spoke to Alex," said David, referring to Alex Theopoulos, Pembroke's chief of police and a good friend to the Lepinsky family, "and he said they've been called in on it."

"You see," said Sebastian, "my hunches are right. There *is* foul play involved."

"Not necessarily. Alex told my father it's probably accidental food poisoning. Where are we going, anyway?"

"Milo's."

David stopped short. "What are we going *there* for?"

Sebastian placed a hand on his friend's shoulder. "You have to promise not to tell anybody," he said.

"Come on, Sebastian. You know me better than that."

Sebastian nodded. "I think this may have been the cause of the poisoning." He reached into his pocket and pulled out a small, white envelope. "It's Miss Swille's secret herbs and spices."

"You think *she* poisoned everybody? Why?"

"I don't know if she did it. In fact, I hope she didn't. All I know is that right before everyone started getting sick, I saw her look at the container in this really strange way."

"Like what?"

Sebastian shook his head. "I can't say exactly. Like . . . troubled. Anyway, I did something bad, David. And this part you *really* can't tell. I took the container."

"You stole it?"

"Calm down. I *borrowed* it. So we could get the contents analyzed, see."

"And that's why we're going to Milo's."

"Right."

"To get the contents analyzed."

"Right."

"And then can we go somewhere and get *me* analyzed?"

"Huh?"

"For going along with these harebrained schemes of yours. Just kidding, Sebastian. Hey, wait a minute, isn't Milo sick?"

"Yeah. We'll just leave it for him so he can take a look at it when he feels better."

When Milo appeared at the front door, he was wearing white pajamas that matched his complexion. "What do you want?" he said.

"Can we come in?" Sebastian asked. "Just for a minute. It's important."

"If we can talk in my room," said Milo, opening the door. "I'm feeling chilled."

"Sure," Sebastian said. David groaned and held his nose, as he reluctantly climbed the stairs.

Moments later, Milo, wrapped in several blankets, examined the contents of Sebastian's envelope. "You think this is what did it?" he said.

"Maybe. You said you wanted to help out, Milo. Do you think you can figure out what's in this mixture?"

"I can try. If I don't have the right books, Mother will, for sure. She's a microbiologist."

"I don't want her involved," said Sebastian.

"She won't be. She has a laboratory and library here at home. I can use them without her knowing. I've done it lots of times. Don't worry about a thing, Barth. Why are you so sure this is the cause of the poisoning, anyway?"

"I'm not," Sebastian said. "All I am sure of is that this poisoning was intentional, not accidental. And when I saw Miss Swille looking at the container of her herbs and spices, I put the two together, that's all. Why was it only the eighth grade that was poisoned? The same food is served to the sixth and seventh grades after all."

"Good question," said David.

"Someone must have put something in the food between lunch periods," Sebastian went on. "Who would have been there to do it?"

"There was Miss Swille," said Milo, "and Mrs. Dribowitz and Mrs. Goode. And, of course, Harley."

David regarded Sebastian for a moment, then said, "And you."

Sebastian smiled. "I was late. By the time I got there, lunch was already being served."

"What's your alibi?"

"I was with you, dummy, remember?"

"Oh, yeah."

"Wait a minute," said Milo, snapping his fingers. "The little devils were there, too."

"Huh?"

"Jason Bruxter and Brad West. I was coming out of gym class when I saw them leaving the kitchen, five minutes before lunch period."

"Are you sure?" Sebastian asked.

"Positive," said Milo, his cheeks regaining some color. "Look, I'll get on this right away. If I can, I'll call you with the results tonight, Barth."

"You're sick, Milo," Sebastian replied. "Tomorrow will be okay."

"Why do you need it by tomorrow?" David asked. "What's wrong with the day after?"

"Did you forget?" said Sebastian. "Tomorrow's Wednesday. We have a show to tape."

26

"I CAN BREATHE AGAIN," David said, as the boys walked away from Milo's house. "One more time in that room and I may never wear my Mickey Mouse T-shirt again. What's he see in mice, anyway?"

"You're hoping to understand Milo Groot?"

"Good point. Where to now?"

"Someone else's house."

"Whose?"

"Harley's."

"Harley's?"

"Yeah. Let's go back and get our bikes."

"He'll beat us up."

"For what?" said Sebastian. "We're just paying a little social call, as Gram would say."

David scratched his head. "Does that mean we should bring something?" he asked. "Cookies? Candy? Chains?"

By the time the boys got to the old stone house off Route 7, it was shrouded in a fine mist, making it look like it belonged on the cover of one of those paperback novels found in supermarket checkout lines. Behind it, gray clouds swirled in an even grayer sky. Sebastian and David dismounted their bicycles hesitantly, neither voicing to the other the half-expectation that they would be met at the door by the Prince of Darkness or, at the least, a deranged governess.

"Let's get this movie straight," David whispered to Sebastian as they waited for their knocking to be answered. "Are we in the middle of some teenage biker epic or *Count Dracula*?"

When the door slowly opened and the yawning, stubbled face of a tiny, withered old man appeared, Sebastian whispered back, "Neither. Try *Snow White and the Seven Dwarfs*."

"Okay, but which one is he—Sleepy or Dopey?"

"What the hell you boys want?" the man barked.

"Grumpy," said Sebastian. "Excuse me, sir. We didn't mean to disturb you, but we're looking for your grandson."

"My grandson? I don't have any." The door started to swing shut.

"Harley?" said Sebastian quickly. "That is, Edward. Edward Davidson?"

"Eddie?" The door was now open just a crack. "Out back. He don't live here. Out back."

"But—"

The door slammed shut.

"I'm glad we didn't bring cookies," David said. "What do you suppose he means by 'out back'?"

"One way to find out," said Sebastian. "Go—"

"Out back. Got it."

As the boys rounded the side of the house, they were met by the sight of a large, run-down barn and adjacent chicken coop. Neither looked as if it had been used in years. "You don't think Harley lives in a chicken coop, do you?" asked David.

"I think it's more likely he lives over there," Sebastian replied, pointing.

On the far side of the barn, in a field that probably once grew corn or oats, was a beat-up house trailer surrounded by even more beat-up looking cars and trucks and motorcycles. "He lives in a cemetery for motor vehicles," said David. "First it's dead mice, now it's dead cars."

The door to the trailer opened, and down the shaky steps came a woman carrying a briefcase. When she spotted the boys, she moved quickly in their direction.

"Hello. Are you friends of Harley's?"

"Yes, ma'am," said Sebastian, in his best talking-to-adults voice. "I'm Sebastian Barth, and this is David Lepinsky. Is Harley okay?"

"Shouldn't he be?" said the woman uncertainly.

"Oh, you know, that poisoning thing at school today and all. That's why we came out. I work with Harley in the kitchen, and I didn't see him after everybody started getting sick. I was afraid he was sick too."

The woman sighed. "I don't think he's sick.

Well, I don't know, to tell you the truth. Do you know where he might be?"

"Isn't he home?"

"No. Do you have any idea where I might find him?" Seeing the boys hesitate, she said, "I'm sorry, I didn't introduce myself. I'm Anne Solomon. I'm a social worker."

"The school called you," said David.

"That's right. How did you know?"

"Oh, just a guess."

"Have you tried the Mobil station?" Sebastian said. "He's there most of the time."

"I went there first. His father said he hadn't seen him. He didn't even realize school had been let out early today."

"No one's at home?"

"His sister Bobbi. She says she hasn't seen him either. But you know his sisters, they'll stick by whatever story he tells them. I'm just worried that he's run away again, the way he did last week." She stopped talking suddenly. "I shouldn't have said that. But as you're friends of his, you know all about it, I'm sure."

"Sure we do," said Sebastian.

"Right," David said.

"Can I give you boys a lift? I'm going to try the gas station again, just in case he's shown up there."

"We have our bikes," Sebastian said. "Thanks, anyway. By the way, Ms. Solomon . . ."

"Yes?"

"I was just wondering something. Harley always told us that the old man in the house was his grandfather. But we never met him before today. He isn't his grandfather, is he?"

"No," said Anne Solomon. "His name is Budge Daniels. He owns the Mobil station where Harley's father works. And he rents them the land here to live on.

"Would you take my card and call me if you hear from Harley? Believe me, you won't be betraying a trust. I want to help him, I think he knows that. Harley's such a bright boy, much brighter than he lets on. A mistake like this could ruin his chances of making things better for himself. Do you understand?"

Sebastian took the social worker's card. "I think so," he said. "We'll let you know if we hear from Harley."

"Thank you. You seem like nice boys. I'm glad to know Harley has friends like you."

27

FRIENDS LIKE YOU.

The phrase kept repeating itself in Sebastian's head during dinner that night. There was something about hearing Ms. Solomon say it, something about the look in her eyes when she did, that made him feel dishonest, the way he had when he'd taken the container of herbs from the cafeteria. He wanted to push the feeling away, but it kept coming back.

"Sebastian isn't with us tonight," said his grandmother.

"Can you blame him?" Katie said. "It's awful, what happened at school today. Thank goodness, Justin Greer is doing much better."

"Is he?" Sebastian asked, coming to.

Katie nodded. "He has to stay in the hospital for more tests. But he's feeling better."

"Do they know what caused it yet?" Jessica asked.

"I spoke to Will fifteen minutes ago. They don't know much."

"Dad's working late?" said Sebastian.

"He should be home in an hour or so. He was going by the hospital to check on Justin and report back to the station. They're covering the story as best they can, but there really isn't much of a story yet. The Board of Health still needs another day to test all the foods that were served at lunch. And the administration, apparently, is being very close-lipped about the entire affair."

Sebastian said, "Really? What's Mr. Hogan saying?"

"Not much, I gather. You can ask your father." Katie glanced at her watch. "I should get back to the restaurant. I have a new evening manager. This is the first night I've left her on her own. I feel like a new mother leaving the baby with the sitter for the first time. I want to call every five minutes and say, 'How is everything?'"

"Then I think you should go down there at once," said Jessica. "Too much worry isn't good for the digestion."

"When Will gets home—"

"Yes, dear, we'll tell him where you are. Run along, run along."

Sebastian tried watching television after dinner, but his mind wasn't on it. His thoughts were in the past, on the trailer behind the old stone house off Route 7, and in the future, on the telephone call he was anticipating from Milo. When he heard the front door open, he jumped up.

"Dad!" he shouted.

Will Barth started to laugh. "I haven't had a

homecoming like that since you were three," he said. "What's up, son?"

"Oh, I was . . . I'm just glad to see you, that's all. I was wondering if you knew anything."

Will's laugh grew. "A little bit," he said. "Less and less as I grow older. But if you mean, do I know anything about the food poisoning at school, I can't say that I do. The Board of Health isn't saying anything yet. And Hap Hogan isn't talking either, which I don't understand at all. He's usually so easygoing; this thing's making a nervous wreck of him. Dottie Swille has her phone off the hook—with good reason, I think. I spoke with her boss at the Department of Food Services, and she is one tough cookie."

"Who? Her boss?"

"Yep. She's new to her position this year, and I think she's hot to prove her stuff. She doesn't understand Dottie's somewhat eccentric style the way the rest of us do, and she's coming down kind of hard on her. The kitchen is being gone over with a fine-tooth comb, she tells me, and if anything is amiss, it could mean Dottie's job."

"Gee," said Sebastian. "Miss Swille's been with the school a long time. They wouldn't really fire her, would they?"

"They might not have a choice," said Will. "Look, son, I'm starved. You want to keep me company while I scramble up some dinner? There's something I need to talk with you about."

"Sure, Dad. There's something I want to ask you too."

Just then, the phone rang. Will picked it up.

"Who?" he said. "Well, there's more than one *Barth* here. Which one did you want?"

Handing the phone to Sebastian, he said, "It's for you. Someone named Milo Groot."

"I've analyzed it," said the voice on the other end of the phone. "Can you come over?"

"Was I right?" Sebastian asked. "Just tell me that."

"A toxic combination of herbs," said Milo. "Not enough to kill anyone, perhaps, but enough to make a lot of people very sick."

"I'll be right over." He put down the receiver.

"Going out, Sebastian?"

"Yeah, Dad, sorry. I've got to go, it's important. Can we talk another time?"

"I suppose we'll have to. What I have to talk about is important too. What did you want to ask me, by the way?"

Sebastian stood framed in the kitchen door. He thought for a minute, then said, "A reporter has an important job to do, doesn't he, Dad?"

Will nodded slowly. "What are you getting at?"

"Well, what I want to know is, what *is* a reporter's job exactly? I mean, what do you see it as?"

"To find the truth and report it."

"As simple as that?"

"As simple as that, although that's far from simple. People have a right to know the truth, Sebastian. A reporter is simply someone who sees that that right is fulfilled."

Sebastian nodded his head slowly. "Thanks, Dad," he said. "I'll see you later. We'll talk then, okay?" He grabbed a jacket, and ran out the front door.

"We'll talk then," Will said to the empty room.

28

"*HEDERA HELIX. Sambucus canadensis. Malus domestica.*" Sebastian lowered the paper, and looked blankly at Milo.

"Those," said Milo, sitting cross-legged on his bed, "are the three culprits."

"Foreign exchange students?" Sebastian said. "I give up, Milo. What are they?"

"They're the ingredients in Miss Swille's secret mixture. *Hedera helix* is the generic for English ivy, a common ground cover, the leaves and berries of which contain the triterpene sapog—"

"Please, Milo, we're talking about English ivy. Speak English."

"The leaves and berries can cause vomiting and diarrhea." Milo held out a tiny particle of something green. "Crushed English ivy leaves."

"Next, the vernacular, or common, name for *sambucus canadensis* is elderberry, a tree that is plentiful in this area and whose bark has been known to cause poisoning in children. Behold, crushed elderberry bark."

"And malus whatever?" asked Sebastian.

"Ah, this one won't surprise you, Barth. *Malus domestica* is nothing more than the common apple." He opened the palm of his hand, and said, "Ground apple seeds. They contain—"

"I know," Sebastian said. "Cyanide. Nice going, Milo. You've accomplished in a few hours what the Board of Health is still trying to figure out."

Milo smiled. "Yes," he said, "but how many ten-year-old geniuses do they have working for them?"

29

THE NEXT MORNING, Sebastian went out on his paper route as usual. When he returned, his mother was waiting for him at the door. *Not* as usual.

"Josh Lepinsky just called," she said. "There's school today."

"School? You've got to be kidding. I was planning on going back to bed."

"No such luck, I'm afraid. Did you have breakfast yet? Good. Then how about washing up while I call the next three parents on the phone tree? And then I'll pack you a lunch."

"Terrific," Sebastian mumbled, climbing the stairs. But by the time he'd reached the landing, his thinking was already beginning to change. Perhaps it wouldn't be so bad to have school today. It would give him a chance to do some more investigating before he taped his program that afternoon.

He imagined his opening words: "Hello again. I'm Sebastian Barth. And this is 'Small Talk.' Tuesday, October the eighth, is a day indelibly etched . . ." *Indelibly etched.* He liked that. "Indelibly etched on the minds of . . . on the memory of a town. For on that

[102]

day, seventy-seven innocent children were cut down in the school cafeteria. To learn the truth about this incredible . . . no, horrendous . . . to learn the truth about this horrendous event and the person responsible, stay tuned."

Person. Or persons. Sebastian still wasn't sure which. To learn the truth, he thought . . . stay tuned.

30

THE PRINCIPAL'S gruff voice over the loudspeaker revealed the lack of a good night's sleep.

"It is incumbent on each and every one of us at Pembroke Middle," he was saying, "to proceed as if nothing out of the ordinary has occurred. The events here yesterday were horrendous, there is no doubt about it . . ." He stole my word, Sebastian thought. "But we must not let a case of accidental food poisoning stand in our way. All four eighth grades will meet in the auditorium as one class. Your teachers will come to you. Sixth and seventh graders will follow their normal schedules. For those who forgot to bring bag lunches, sandwiches and milk are being provided by the PTA and may be picked up at the office. You should report to your homerooms for lunch period, since the cafeteria is closed.

"Now, there may be some newspaper and television people on the premises today. Please be courteous to them. You need not, however, I repeat, you need *not* answer their questions. Should you find that they are intrusive in any way, please come to the office and report the matter to Mrs. Kershaw or myself at once. Thank you. What, Sandy? Oh, yes. Please stand for the pledge."

Accidental food poisoning, Sebastian thought, as he placed his hand over his heart. What's Mr. Hogan trying to hide? Or: who is he protecting?

". . . with liberty and justice for all."

Later, during a free period, Sebastian removed his bookbag from his locker and made his way to the cafeteria. Through a window in the double doors, he could see Bea Goode and Lillian Dribowitz playing cards. He knocked.

"Sebastian," Bea said, opening the door, "you're not supposed to be here."

"I know," he said. "I just wanted to see how everybody was doing. Is Dottie here?"

Bea shook her head sadly. "Poor thing," she said. "She's taking it so hard. Lil and I came in, even though there's nothing for us to do. Somebody's got to be here to answer questions and show the health inspector around, I suppose. The health inspector and that Mrs. Shea."

"Who's she?"

"The new director of food services. Lordy, but she's a tough nut."

Sebastian smiled. "My dad said she's a tough cookie," he said.

"Tough nut, tough cookie, there are other things

[105]

I could call her if you weren't too young to hear 'em. She's inspecting this place like she's the drill sergeant and we're the new recruits."

"Be careful what you say about her," said Lillian Dribowitz, dealing herself a hand of solitaire. "She's my cousin."

"That so?" said Bea.

Lillian nodded. "Second cousin, once removed, but family's family."

"Family may be family," Bea said, pursing her lips, "but it seems to me she's being a little insensitive about this whole thing."

"She's thorough, that's all," Lillian said. She looked up from her cards. "Are you forgetting all those children who were poisoned yesterday? In *this* cafeteria? Is she being insensitive to them?"

Bea sighed. "You're right, I know," she said. "It's Dottie I'm thinking of. I just hate to see this happen to her. She's given twenty-five years to this school. I don't know what effect all this will have, but it can't be good.

"What she didn't want to tell you, Sebastian, is that there's a big dinner planned in her honor in January. She got wind of it, and was so excited. She's never been at the center of attention, you know, not once in her life. And now it seems that she never will be, not even when she deserves it most."

"I've worked for the school district for twenty-

six years," said Lillian softly. "You don't see me making a fuss."

"For the district," said Bea. "Not for the same school. Besides, you took time out for your children."

"Twenty-six years is twenty-six years," Lillian said.

"And family is family," said Bea.

Lillian had all four aces out, and was running out of cards in her hand. "It looks like you're going to win," Sebastian said.

"You might say so," said Lillian Dribowitz.

31 "I COULDN'T get rid of it," Sebastian
told David, as the two gathered their belongings after school. He tapped the bulge
in his bookbag. "There was no way to get past Bea
or Mrs. Dribowitz. Now I really am concealing
evidence."

"Nice move."

"Tell me again everything you heard in the office, will you? I need to put the pieces in place before
we tape."

"Couldn't you delay taping, Sebastian? Just this
once?"

"You know how the station works. We've got our
scheduled slot in the studio, and that's it."

"Then put the story off until next week. We've
got the beekeeper for fifteen minutes. Keep him on
for all thirty, or put Uncle Harry on the show again."

"David—"

"All I'm saying is, don't jump the gun. You
don't know the whole story yet. You have to give
people a chance."

"You have to give people the truth," said Sebastian. "Tell me again, David. Everything."

David shook his head and sighed. "Okay. The Board of Health report confirms your—correction, Milo's—findings. Those weird crushed plants and things were ground up in the food. No one—no one but you and me, that is—knows where they came from. Miss Swille told them that she uses a combination of herbs and spices, which she keeps in a plastic container on a shelf over the oven. And she told them the ingredients."

"What were they?"

"I don't remember. Some stuff that sounded like orangutan and margarine, something like that. It doesn't matter. What matters is she said that she noticed right before everybody got sick that her container was missing and an identical one had been put in its place."

Sebastian grabbed his friend's arm. "You didn't tell me that."

"I didn't? I guess I forgot."

"You *can't* forget details like that. The entire container was replaced, that's important. Do they have suspects?"

"Miss Swille says she doesn't remember who was in or out of the kitchen between lunch periods yesterday. All she can account for are herself, the other two kitchen ladies and Harley. Oh yeah, and Jason and Brad, who had to sweep up the cafeteria because they'd been caught horsing around in the hall. But she says there was some problem about deliveries being left down the hall earlier, so she and the others had to keep leaving the kitchen to go get things."

"In other words," said Sebastian, "somebody could have come and gone without the others noticing."

David nodded. "It's possible," he said. "But that isn't what it looks like."

"What do you mean?" Sebastian asked. "Is there something else you forgot to tell me?"

"Not really. It's just that Harley's still missing."

"So everybody's assuming he did it. I wish we could talk to him. I hate to go on the air without—"

"Are you boys still here? There are no after-school activities today, you know." Sebastian and David looked up to see the school secretary walking toward them. She adjusted her cardigan sweater, which was about to slip off one shoulder.

"We're going, Mrs. Kershaw," said David. "We were just talking about Harley. He hasn't been found, has he?"

A funny expression came over Mrs. Kershaw's face. "Not exactly," she said. "But the police are out looking for him now."

"Missing person?" Sebastian asked.

"More like *wanted*. His sister told them that Harley called her."

"And?"

"And he's confessed to the whole thing."

32

"LOOKS LIKE you've got your story," David said, pushing open the radio station door. The boys were met by a blast of frigid air. "Geez, what's going on in here?"

The receptionist looked up from her desk, where she sat wrapped in two sweaters, a down coat and a half-knitted afghan, trailing a ball of yarn. "There's something wrong with the hoozis in here," she said. "The rest of the place is warm as toast."

"Thermostat?"

"Whatever. Sebastian, dear heart, your father wants to see you."

"What about, Denise?"

"How should I know? Have you been a bad boy lately?"

"No worse than usual."

"Well, all I can tell you is he wants to see you pronto."

Just then, Harry Dobbs shuffled into the room. When he saw the boys, he didn't say hello. He didn't even smile.

"You okay, Uncle Harry?" Sebastian said.

[111]

"Change, change," Harry muttered.

"What?" said David.

"Everything has to change. Why? That's what I want to know, why?"

"Why do things have to change?" asked Sebastian, trying to make sense of Harry's question.

Harry nodded. "Do you know why I called my program 'A Few Raisins'? It's an odd name for a radio show, don't you think?"

Sebastian smiled and said, "I'm used to it. It seems normal enough to me."

"It's from the writer, O. Henry," Harry went on. " 'Inject,' he said, 'a few raisins of conversation into the tasteless dough of existence.' Raisins, apparently, are no longer in fashion. Instead, we mold the tasteless bread of existence into a loaf that will please the eye even as it deadens the palate and provides no nourishment whatsoever."

Sebastian glanced at David. "Excuse me, Uncle Harry," he said, "I think I have to talk with my father."

The sound of darts landing with a heavy thunk-thunk-thunk echoed down the hallway, as the two friends moved quickly to the station manager's office.

"I'm sorry," Will Barth said moments later. He still held a dart in one hand; the other hand had settled, somewhat uncomfortably, on his son's shoulder. "Herself laid down the law yesterday."

"I know," said Sebastian. "So you had to cancel

Uncle Harry's show. But do you have to fire him, Dad?"

Will was caught momentarily off guard. Recovering himself, he said, "I'm not firing Harry, Sebastian. I'm not even cancelling his show, for that matter."

"You're not?"

"No. Herself wanted me to, but I convinced her to give him a three-month probation period to push the ratings up. The name and format are going to have to be changed, of course."

"What's the show going to be called now?"

" 'The Harry Dobbs Show.' "

"Catchy."

"It was her suggestion. She said it provided a clearer market identity. So be it. Son, what I needed to talk with you about isn't Harry's show. It's yours." Sebastian felt himself stiffen under his father's touch. "This isn't easy for me. Herself insisted that your program be cancelled as well, but . . . wait a minute, now . . . I got us four weeks to give her what she wants."

"Which is what?" said Sebastian.

"More impact. A sense of the here and now. Immediacy."

"Immediacy?"

"She says the programs haven't been relevant."

"Dad, Pembroke's a small town. There isn't that much happening."

"You have to look harder then. Don't go for the obvious. Find the story beneath the story. You can do that, Sebastian, I've seen you do it. David, you're the writer for the show. We'll all work together. I'm not happy about this, boys, but we have to give Herself what she asks for. She pays the bills, so she calls the shots."

"Well, if it's immediacy she wants," Sebastian said to David, as the two walked determinedly down the hall to Studio B, "it's immediacy she's going to get."

33

"YOU DID IT," David said to Sebastian, the moment the beekeeper left them and the red light went off outside Studio B. The show was taped and ready to air at seven that evening. "You're either real brave or real stupid."

"Why?" Sebastian said. "I told the truth. Nothing brave or stupid about it. I just did it before anyone else did, that's all. And unless somebody spills the beans within the next two hours, I'll have the story on the air first."

"A scoop," said David.

"Immediacy," said Sebastian, pushing through the swinging doors into the reception area.

"It's *freezing* in here," David said.

Noticing that they weren't alone, Sebastian called out, "Aren't you cold, Uncle Harry?"

Harry Dobbs looked up from where he sat huddled in a chair. "I'm keeping myself warm, boys. Don't you worry about me."

"He's drinking," David whispered.

"You want to walk home with us?" said Sebastian.

"That's all right," Harry answered, waving his

hand. "I've got some thinking to do. You go ahead."

Outside, Sebastian said, "Dad'll make sure he's okay. He won't let him drive home like that. I just wish he wouldn't drink. You want to come over for a while?"

"I can't. Dad's taking Rachel and me out to the mall to buy new ice skates."

"A little early in the year, isn't it?"

"There's a sale. You want to come?"

"No, thanks. I think I'll go home and do some of what Uncle Harry's doing."

"You're going home to drink?"

"Think," said Sebastian. "I'm going home to think."

"What for? You've solved the case. There's nothing left to think about."

Sebastian picked up a stone and tossed it in his hand. "I wonder," he said.

34

SEBASTIAN ROAMED the empty house, back and forth past curious cat eyes, looking for something to do. He'd wanted to think, but now it seemed he wanted only to avoid his thoughts. He drank half a glass of milk, pushed the buttons on the remote control, read the same first sentence of the same book over and over.

After awhile, he picked up the phone and dialed David's number, then remembered that no one would be home. He called Corrie next, but she wasn't home either.

"She's at the old ballfield," Ginny Wingate told him. "The one out on Route 7."

"Oh," said Sebastian.

"Shall I tell her you called?"

"That's okay. But I'd like to talk with Reverend Wingate if he's there."

"I'm afraid he isn't. He's over at the hospital visiting the boy who took so ill. He'll be home by six. Shall I have him call you? Is there anything I can do?"

"No, that's all right. Bye."

"Goodbye, Sebastian."

Sebastian raised the flap of the bookbag lying

next to the phone and pulled out his notebooks, being careful to leave the plastic container of herbs tucked away inside. He realized he hadn't looked at the new *Paragon*.

"I wonder what Milo's editorial is this week," he said aloud, flipping the newspaper to the center page. He was surprised to see that there was none. In its place was the petition Milo had circulated, calling on the administration to take action against the gangs, which were "growing in the student body like a cancer run amok." Sebastian flinched at the wording and the exaggeration. The gangs supposedly running amok were in fact only one gang, consisting of three students. And even that gang wouldn't be around much longer. It was almost certain Harley would not be returning to school, and Jason and Brad, left on their own, would surely return to their former selves, just as Adam had predicted.

Sebastian looked at the petition again. Milo had managed to collect only three signatures. It looked more like a letter to the editor than a petition. It made him angry to see his name at the top of the list:

Sebastian Barth
Justin Greer
Lindsay Carmichael

His anger turned suddenly to pity. Poor Milo. He was such a twerp. Here he was editor of the school paper, and he could find only three people to sign his petition. Nobody liked Milo Groot. Nobody, thought Sebastian, but his mother. And Brian Hansen. And maybe his mice.

He folded the newspaper and stuck it in his pocket. Grabbing an apple from the bowl on the kitchen table and his jacket from the hook on the door, he started out. He'd get his bike and ride, he decided. There was a place he liked to go to be alone; perhaps his thoughts would come more clearly there.

35

ON THE WAY, he passed the field where Corrie and her friends were playing football.

"Corrie!" he called out.

"Sebastian, what are you doing here?" Corrie called time out, and ran to the spot where Sebastian stood straddling his bicycle.

"Just out for a ride," said Sebastian. "How's the game?"

"Great," Corrie said, catching her breath. "Guess what? I have the best news."

"They're letting you on the team?"

"Better. They're letting me start a *new* team, an official school team."

"Like the Panthers?"

"Yep. If you can't join them, beat them. We're the Pembroke Pandas, the first official middle school all-girl football team in the state of Connecticut."

"Hey," said Sebastian. "That's all right. I'm impressed."

"Really?"

"Yeah, I am. When did you become official?"

"Today. Mr. Hogan got the go-ahead from the

coach and the school superintendent. We probably would have known yesterday, but Mr. Turman was out sick, remember? No gym classes."

"That's right," said Sebastian, his mind suddenly on something else. "No gym classes. I've gotta go, Corrie."

"Don't you want to stay and watch us play?"

"Another time. I have the feeling I'll have lots of chances. And if you need a head cheerleader, I'm your man."

"Thanks," Corrie said, with a laugh.

That is, Sebastian thought, as he pedaled away, if I'm not kicked out of school first.

36

SEBASTIAN DROPPED his bike at the same spot he usually did when he came here, by the rusting wrought-iron fence that had once been the gateway to what must have been a large and impressive estate. The house, stone like Budge Daniel's and many of the others along Route 7, had burned to the ground years earlier, leaving only a shell. The remaining stones and charred beams were wrapped in vines, buried in leaves and weeds and shadows.

Sebastian made his way through the woods as silently as possible, afraid, almost, to disturb the ghosts that inhabited the place. He was eager to get to the high-backed stone bench, set away from the house in what had probably been a garden, where he often came to sit and think and be alone. Something wasn't right, he kept telling himself. There were pieces that didn't fit the puzzle, and the ones that did, fit too easily. He glanced at his watch. Ten minutes to six. His program would be on the air in a little over an hour. What if he'd been wrong?

Looking up from his watch, he stopped himself short. Someone was sitting on his bench. He couldn't make out who it was; nor, apparently, could the person see him clearly. But when they spoke, they recognized each other at once.

"Biker, is that you?" said the figure on the bench.

"Harley?"

"Sebastian?"

"Harley, what are you doing here? Everybody's looking for you. The police—"

"The police?" Harley jumped up as Sebastian walked quickly and noisily toward him, forsaking now the ghosts for the living.

"Yeah," said Sebastian. He brought himself to a halt several yards away from where Harley stood, his eyes wide and staring like a frightened deer's. "They said you confessed."

"*Who* said so?" Harley asked, not moving.

"Your sister."

"My sister? Which one?"

"I don't know, Harley. I just heard—"

"Geez," said Harley, dropping back down onto the bench. "It must have been Suzanne." His clothes, the plaid button-down shirt and khaki chinos, were wrinkled and dirty, the Hush Puppies coated with mud. Sebastian noticed that Harley had stacked his school books at one end of the bench; he wondered if they were serving as a pillow.

"Aren't you cold out here?" he asked.

"Yeah, I'm cold," Harley said bitterly. He lay back and closed his eyes, taking himself somewhere

Sebastian couldn't follow. After a time, he said, "Biker was supposed to be bringing me some stuff, a jacket, some stuff. I thought you were him. He ain't coming."

"Did you sleep here last night?"

"Over there," said Harley, with a slight nod to a nearby storage shed.

"It must have been real cold then," Sebastian said.

"It was all right."

"Are you running away?"

Harley's eyes popped open. "You my social worker or something?"

"No, but I saw her. She's really worried."

"Is that why you came here, Sebastian?"

"No. I didn't know you were here. I didn't think anybody knew about this place but me."

"So why are you here?"

Sebastian, tired of standing, hunkered down onto his haunches. "I had some thinking to do," he said. "I come here to think sometimes."

"Me too," said Harley. "I guess we just never did our thinking at the same time. So what did you come here to think about?"

"The stuff that's been happening at school."

"The puking?"

"The poisoning," said Sebastian. "Did you do it, Harley?"

Harley looked at Sebastian as if he were the biggest fool God ever made. "If they say I did, then I guess I did."

"You didn't do it," Sebastian said, as much to himself as Harley. "So why did you confess?"

Harley closed his eyes again and waited a long time to answer. "I didn't confess," he said.

"But your sister—"

"Suzanne's a jerk. I told her what I just told you. It doesn't matter if I did it or not, everybody's going to think I did. So I may as well take the blame."

"But that isn't what you're doing," said Sebastian. "You're running away."

"Yeah, well, I learned good." For a time, the crickets made the only conversation. Then, Harley spoke softly. "My mom, she run away a long time ago. I never seen her since I was six. And my dad, well, he's just always running away. The difference is he comes back."

"Were you planning to come back?"

"I don't know. What have I got to come back to?"

"Your sisters," said Sebastian. "Your dad. Your friends."

"Right. Now you really sound like my social worker."

"Sorry. I didn't mean to. I just—"

"She says, that social worker, she says if my dad don't get his act together and stop his drinking and all that, if he don't stop his running away whenever he's got problems, she's going to have to put us all in foster homes. It's happened before, it won't be the first time. But she says it might be the last."

Sebastian opened his mouth, but said nothing. He wasn't sure what there was to say. Besides, it seemed as if Harley had more of a need to talk all of a sudden than to listen.

"My dad, he joined the AA over the summer and me, I got into the creative arts program at the center. It was pretty dumb, but I did it because the Solomon lady said I should. And I believed her. Stupid. She said I'd make new friends. Well, she was right about that. That's where I hooked up with Biker and Breeze. Like I said: Stupid.

"When school started, she told me I should be a volunteer. Try helping, she said, instead of hurting. So I went to work in the cafeteria. I figured I could save up my lunch money for Christmas. But, hey, I might not even have a family by Christmas, you know?"

Harley's voice grew even quieter; Sebastian found himself straining to hear each word.

"That Solomon, she told me I'm too smart to throw myself away. That's what she says I'm doing, throwing myself away. She says I'm only thirteen, I got a whole life ahead of me. She says, everybody makes mistakes. She says, you make a mistake on the blackboard, what do you do? You erase it and try again. I say to her, sometimes somebody writes on the blackboard with a magic marker, just to be mean, and everybody sees it and nobody can erase it away. It's always there, and always will be the rest of your life."

"Come on," Sebastian said. "Don't be so hard on yourself, Harley. Everybody makes mistakes."

Harley started to laugh. "What kind of mistakes do you make?" he said. "You put on a sweater that don't match your shirt and have to live with it the rest of the day? Give me a break. You're popular, Sebastian. You don't know what it's like to be on the outside."

"It seems to me," said Sebastian, "that Jason and Brad wanted to be your friends just because you were on the outside. They wanted to be like you."

Harley opened his eyes slowly. They were red around the rims. "Yeah," he said, "well, you want a surprise? I want to be like them. But it don't work that way. They came here before, 'cause they know I hang out here sometimes, and they told me they can't be Devil Riders no more. I said, why? They said their moms told 'em they couldn't. I said, go home to your mommies then. But bring me a coat, some stuff. I'm cold out here. They ain't coming back, you know why? Not because their moms told them they couldn't. That's bull. They ain't coming back because being my friend means trouble now. They liked looking tough, but they're not so good at being tough. They haven't had the practice, like me.

"It's okay," said Harley, sitting up. "I don't need

[127]

them. And I don't need no social worker. And I don't need you here, Sebastian, with that dopey look on your face."

"I guess I'm feeling sorry for you," said Sebastian.

Harley's body tightened up. "Don't. Just get out of here and leave me alone."

"But—"

"Sorry if you needed the place to do some thinking, but I got here first."

Sebastian stood and rubbed the back of his aching knees. "Are you still going to run away?"

"Sure."

"But why?"

"You're really dumb, Sebastian."

"But if you didn't do it—"

"Who said I didn't do it?"

"I don't understand."

"Will it make you feel better if you get a real confession out of me? Okay. I confess."

"What?"

"You heard me. I confess. I did it. Why not? I hate everybody in that stinking, rotten school. They've always treated me like a piece of cow dung they couldn't get off their shoes. So I finally got even. I'm glad I did it, and I'm glad I told you. But, hey, if you're thinking of running back and telling the police where to look, forget it. I'll be long gone by the time they get here."

Feeling there was nothing left to be said, Sebastian removed his jacket and tossed it to Harley. It landed at his feet.

"Hey!" Harley called, as Sebastian started back through the woods.

"Keep it," Sebastian called back over his shoulder. "It's supposed to get a lot colder tonight."

He made it to Corrie's house in under ten minutes. Waiting at the door, he checked his watch. Six-twenty-five.

"Well, Sebastian," said Corrie's father, letting him in. "Mrs. Wingate told me you called."

"Reverend Wingate, do you remember that time I asked you about people hurting each other?"

"I do."

"You said you'd give it thought, and we could talk about it again some time."

"I have given it thought," Reverend Wingate said. "And dinner won't be ready for awhile yet. Shall we talk now?"

"I'd like that," said Sebastian.

37

THE DOOR SLAMMED. His feet pounded the stairs. "Is that you, Sebastian?" his grandmother called. The moment he reached his bedroom, he yanked the newspaper out of his pocket and looked at it again. It was all so clear. Why hadn't he seen it? He pulled a sweatshirt over his head, and shoved the paper back into place.

Down the stairs. Into the kitchen. Call David.

There was no answer. "He still isn't home," Sebastian said.

"Why, it's almost seven," said his grandmother. "Shall we listen to your program together?"

"I can't this time, Gram. Sorry."

"Your parents should be home shortly," his grandmother called after him. "Dinner will be at seven-thirty. I've made one of your—"

"I'll be back soon." The door slammed. His feet pounded the sidewalk. He glanced at his watch. Five to seven. Hurry. It's the beginning of the show he has to hear. It's the conviction without trial. That's the thing. Hurry.

He reached the front door at exactly one minute

to seven. The refrain from the 1812 hadn't finished when the door swung open.

"Barth!"

"Hi, Milo. We don't have time to talk. There's something I want you to hear. Do you have a radio in your room?"

"Of course. Several. The best reception is on the one I built when I was six. However—"

"Great. Let's go."

"But I'm eating dinner."

"Later, Milo. This is important."

"Milo, who is it?" Mrs. Groot's voice entered the room like an angry bee. "If that's Brian Hansen, you just tell him—"

"It's Barth, Mom."

"Oh, hello, Sebastian." The bee found honey. "Won't you join us for dinner?"

Sebastian didn't reply. He hadn't heard. He had pushed Milo up the stairs and gotten him to turn on the radio just in time to hear, "Hello again. I'm Sebastian Barth. And this is 'Small Talk.' "

"You want me to hear your show, Barth? Why?"

"I figured you deserved to, Milo. You were such an important part in helping me get my story. Listen."

Milo sat on the edge of his bed. Sebastian leaned against a dresser.

". . . a situation that had the school administration and the Board of Health baffled until today," Sebastian's voice was saying through the radio speaker. "Was it a flu epidemic, as was first believed? Or, if it was food poisoning, was it accidental or deliberate?

"While the administration and the Board of Health charted their course on bureaucratic waters—"

"Nice turn of phrase," said Milo.

"That's David's," Sebastian said. "He's good at that sort of thing."

". . . with the help of fellow students, Milo Groot and David Lepinsky, and this is what I've learned: A toxic combination of natural herbs and plants was introduced into the food by an eighth-grade student, Edward Davidson. Davidson, who had been working as a volunteer in the cafeteria, has confessed to the crime, although his motive and his present whereabouts are unknown. It is unlikely that Dorothy Swille, cafeteria manager, was aware of what Davidson, known in the school as 'Harley,' was doing. Still, though she is essentially blameless, she must share the responsibility. So, it would seem, must the school principal, Eugene Hogan, who denied there was a problem until seventy-seven children were stricken down, one of whom, Justin Greer, is still in the hospital."

"That's telling it like it is," Milo said. His cheeks were flushed with excitement.

"I thought you'd like it," said Sebastian, clicking off the radio.

"Wait, I want to hear the rest."

"Oh, I just went on and on like that," Sebastian said. "I was really hot. But you get the idea. I held Harley responsible, and Miss Swille, and the school administration. I even went on to point a finger at the Board of Health. It's amazing what you can do when you're convinced you're telling the truth. I blamed just about everybody. Everybody, that is, but the one person who really deserved it."

Milo gave Sebastian an odd look, but said nothing.

"How did Fritzie die, Milo?"

"What?"

Sebastian nodded toward a cage where several mice competed for the use of an exercise wheel. "Fritzie," he said, "your favorite mouse. How did she die?"

"What are you getting at, Barth? I don't know how she died. Old age, I suppose."

"You know, Milo, David asked me once what you saw in mice. I couldn't answer him, but now I think I can. Every inch of this room is a laboratory. You don't just keep mice as pets, you experiment with them. Isn't that box over there a maze?"

Milo shrugged. "So?"

"I was just wondering if Fritzie died from one of your experiments."

"You've been watching too much television. I

don't know the point of all this, and I don't see what it has to do with your radio show or with the poisoning at school."

"It has everything to do with both of them, Milo, and you know it. You're bright, maybe you're even a genius like the sign on your door says. But could you really have figured out so quickly what it took the Board of Health almost two days to discover?"

"Why not? They had to sort through all those different foods, after all. I had the actual toxic agents. *You* gave them to me."

"After *you* left them in the school kitchen. Apple seeds, anyone could get a hold of those. English ivy, it's all over the place, including the border along your front walk. And elderberry trees, well, Milo, you yourself said they're popular in this area, although not quite as popular as you might like to think. You have a nice one out back. Isn't that where your mom gets the berries for her jam?"

"Please, Barth," Milo said, standing. "Your defective detective work is beginning to bore me. *Anyone* could have figured out how to put those ingredients together. Anyone could have found them if, as we both agree, they are so plentiful."

"Not everyone has your imagination or your gift for research and experimentation."

"So I killed my favorite mouse in the name of science?"

"I didn't say you killed her on purpose. Sometimes, experiments go wrong. And I didn't say you did anything in the name of science. No, what you did, you did for revenge."

"Revenge? For what?"

"For all the times Harley humiliated you, especially that time at the awards assembly last spring. For all the times the rest of the kids laughed at you. For all the times you've felt like an outsider."

Milo's head jerked back slightly, as if he'd been slapped. "I haven't just felt like an outsider, Barth. I *am* an outsider. You don't know what that's like. You're popular. You don't know how much it hurts, knowing that no one likes you, knowing that your only friend is someone you don't even like, but whose friendship you tolerate because it's all you can get."

"So you poison your classmates and set it up for Harley to take the blame. Very clever. You had me convinced. It looks like everyone else is convinced now, too."

Milo began to wipe his hands on his pants. "Don't be idiotic, Barth. You seem to forget that I was the first one poisoned, that in fact I have been poisoned three times. Would I poison myself?"

"As I said, Milo, you're very clever. You conducted a little experiment on yourself. You wanted to learn just how sick your little mixture would make someone. Someone human, that is; you'd already found out what it could do to a mouse. While you were at it, you established yourself as a victim. And who would suspect the victim of being the culprit?"

"Really, this is ridiculous."

"I have to admire you," Sebastian said. Milo smiled in spite of himself. "Not that I like what you did, but you certainly were good at it. You put some of the stuff in your own food, not once, but twice; then, when you were circulating your petition, you sneaked a little into the food of the two people who took the time to sign." Sebastian removed the *Paragon* from his pocket and pointed to the signatures below his. "Probably," he said, "the clipboard you were carrying covered their plates while they were signing. Justin Greer and Lindsay Carmichael helped you out, and you thanked them . . . with a little poison. Once you saw the effect on them, you were ready to move on to the big time."

"And how did I do that?" Milo asked, continuing to wipe his hands on his pants.

"You watched outside the kitchen until the coast was clear, then sneaked in and switched plastic containers. Easy enough to do with the kind of container found in almost any store. And luck was on your side. Because of the way deliveries were made yesterday, Miss Swille and the others were in and out of the kitchen a lot."

"And how did I have the luxury to stand around and wait for just the right opportunity? Did school go into suspended animation all of a sudden? I have gym class before lunch, Barth."

"Ordinarily, you have gym class, Milo. Yesterday, there were no gym classes, remember? Mr. Turman was absent. You had a free period. You slipped when you told me you'd been coming from gym and saw Jason and Brad in the cafeteria. It's true, they were there. But you saw them because you'd been standing outside watching them for some time.

"The only thing I'm still not sure of is how you knew about Miss Swille's secret herbs and spices in the first place. But I figure anybody who tries to impress teachers as much as you do has probably been a runner to the cafeteria lots of times. Once you'd thought up your little scheme, you just looked around for the best way to make it happen."

"All of this is interesting speculation," said Milo. "But you can't prove a thing by it."

"That's true," Sebastian replied. "It will take a confession to settle things once and for all. Harley has confessed because he feels it's expected of him and he has nothing to lose. Of course, the truth is that he has everything to lose—a chance for a new beginning for himself and his family, for starters. And Miss Swille, by implication, will have her reputation hurt. She'll lose her big twenty-fifth anniversary party, for sure. I stand to lose something, too."

Milo snorted.

"Don't laugh," said Sebastian. "I went on the

air and told lies. I didn't know I was doing it, but that's no excuse. I didn't have all the evidence. I was too eager to get a scoop, too worried about saving my show. When the truth comes out—and it will come out, Milo, one way or another—I could lose a lot."

"*If* the truth comes out," Milo said slowly, "or what you *call* the truth, I stand to lose too. They might make me resign as editor of the school paper. That may not seem like much to you, Barth, but it means a lot to me."

"I know it does. Each of us stands to lose something that means a lot, Milo. The difference is that you're guilty and we're not. And you're the only one who can make it come out right."

"And if I don't? Presuming my guilt, that is."

"If you don't, then I'll have to do whatever I can to clear my own name and the names of everyone I wrongly accused on my show. By the way, I still have the container."

Milo's hands stopped moving. He sat very still and listened.

"I have a lot of apologizing to do," Sebastian continued. "To Harley and Miss Swille, to Mr. Hogan and my father. And to my listeners, Milo. I owe them all an apology. And I owe them the truth."

"The truth," said Milo, "hurts sometimes."

"Agreed," Sebastian said. "But it can make things better too. Not like poison. Poison just makes you sick, and it leaves a bitter taste." He started toward the door, then turned back. "Eat your poison, Milo," he said. And he quietly left the room.

Milo didn't move for a long time. He just sat and watched the mice spin their wheels round and round. And then, without even realizing it was happening at first, he began to cry.

"Fritzie," he said. "I'm sorry."

What is the secret of the
ghost in the cemetery?

An exciting preview of
Sebastian Barth's
spine-tingling first case

What Eric Knew

by

JAMES HOWE

1 THE FIRST THING Sebastian Barth heard when he woke that summer morning was mail being pushed through the slot in the front door and landing with a soft thud inside. From the sound, it was a two-magazine day, he decided. He yawned and rolled over in bed. The clock read ten past nine. Sebastian smiled at the luxury of sleeping so late.

Stretching, he reached for his robe and headed downstairs. The house was still. His father had probably left for the radio station at least an hour before. And his mother would be at the farmers' market buying fresh vegetables for her restaurant. As for Gram, he couldn't guess where she was this morning. Sebastian's grandmother had so many "worthy causes," as she called them, that "there weren't enough hours in the day."

When he entered the kitchen, his two cats. Boo and Chopped Liver, attacked his ankles and purred loudly.

"Give me a break, you guys," he said. "You've been fed already."

Chopped Liver flashed him a we-won't-tell-any-body-if-you-feed-us-again sort of look, but Sebastian just shook his head and poured himself a bowl of cereal.

A newspaper lay open on the kitchen table. He noticed a story about some rare books being stolen from a library in New Haven, read about half of it, and turned to the comics.

The phone rang.

"Hey, it's you."

Sebastian recognized the voice of his best friend, David, who lived across the street. "Were you expecting a wrong number?" he asked.

"I didn't think you'd be back from your route yet. You coming over?"

"I didn't have to do my route today. And sure I'm coming over. How was the game?"

"Good. What do you want to do today?"

"I don't know. What do you want to do?"

"I don't know. You want to do some biking?"

"Maybe. But right now I want to rescue my cereal from terminal sogginess. I'll be over in a half hour."

"Okay," David said. And then, as Sebastian was about to hang up, he added, "It's been kind of quiet around here since Eric moved, hasn't it?"

"Yeah," Sebastian said. "Eric did have a way of keeping things lively. At least he did before . . . you know."

"Yeah. Well, see you later."

"See you later."

After he hung up the phone, Sebastian remembered the mail. He'd been right. There were two magazines. There was also something for him. The thin envelope showed no return address, just a Boston postmark. And inside was the strangest letter he had ever received.

2

SEBASTIAN showed the letter to David. It read, "S.I.S."

"That's it?"

Sebastian nodded.

"Who's it from? Wait, don't tell me—Eric, of course."

The two boys were walking down Chestnut Street, toward the house where Eric used to live.

"But what's it mean?" David asked, when Sebastian remained silent. "Hey, look. Someone's moved in."

"I know. I met them yesterday when you were at the game. There's a kid our age."

David regarded Eric's old house with new interest. "What's he like?" he asked.

"You'll see."

A slim woman with short, gray hair stood on the front porch of the house calling, "Buster! Buster!"

"Buster!" David snorted. "What kind of name is that? Gee, Sebastian, that's not the kid, is it? Buster?"

"Don't worry," said Sebastian, as a child ran past them and into the yard, "you won't become the laughingstock of Pembroke because you've got a friend named Buster. That's the kid's little brother. *That's* the kid."

Sebastian pointed toward the garage next to the house. Someone in shorts and a halter top was hosing down a garbage pail.

"A girl?" David said incredulously. The new kid waved and ran toward them. "You didn't tell me . . . oh, great. Just what we need, a *girl*." He made a fist and said, "Curse you, Eric Mather."

"Hi," said the girl, as her sneakers brought her to a squeaky halt. She had a thicket of red hair and a face busy with freckles. When she smiled at Sebastian, her braces sparkled.

"Hi," said Sebastian. "This is my friend, David Lepinsky."

David mumbled something.

"And this is Corrie. . . ."

"Wingate," said Corrie. "Hi, David. What are you guys up to?"

"Well, actually," said Sebastian, "we've got a mystery on our hands. Or sort of a mystery, anyway." Sebastian gave Corrie Eric's letter.

"What are you *doing*?" David hissed.

"Relax. She's okay."

"What's it mean?" Corrie asked, handing the letter back to Sebastian.

"I'm not sure, but I have a hunch."

"Sebastian always has a hunch," David said.

"I think it has something to do with the way Eric was acting before he left."

"Eric? Oh yeah, the kid who used to live here." Corrie picked at a mosquito bite on her leg. "How was he acting?"

"Weird," said Sebastian.

David nodded. "Definitely weird," he said.

Sebastian went on, "Eric was always . . . well, adventurous, I guess you could say. He liked . . ."

"Getting into trouble," David said.

"Something like that. He liked having a good time, goofing around, nosing into other people's business. You know?"

"I think so. But what's weird about that?"

"Nothing. It's just that he changed a few weeks before he moved. All of a sudden, he got kind of quiet and kept to himself. When we asked him what was going on, he didn't want to talk about it. Said he *couldn't* talk about it. And then, about three days before he moved, he fell down a flight of stairs and broke his leg."

"Wow," said Corrie, as her picking drew blood. "How come?"

"How come what?" asked David.

"How come he fell down the stairs?"

"We don't know," Sebastian said. "He wouldn't tell us. But he hinted that he'd been pushed."

"Wow," Corrie said again.

"And now this," said Sebastian, holding up Eric's letter. "S.I.S."

"Are they somebody's initials?"

"Seems like it," Sebastian said.

"But we don't know anybody with those initials," said David.

"Well, I can think of one person." Sebastian paused and then said, "Susan Iris Siddons."

David looked at him as if he'd gone nuts.

"And you think maybe it was Susan Siddons who pushed Eric down the stairs?" asked Corrie.

"I have a hunch that's what Eric's trying to tell us," Sebastian said. "There's just one little problem."

"Definitely," said David.

"What?" Corrie asked.

Sebastian looked past Corrie's house to the cemetery in its shadow. "Susan Siddons died in 1902," he said.

OTHER BOOKS
BY JAMES HOWE